MURDER
&
THE MOVIE STAR

A Cedar Bay Cozy Mystery - Book 12

BY

DIANNE HARMAN

Published by: Dianne Harman
www.dianneharman.com

Interior, cover design and website by
Vivek Rajan

ISBN: 978-1545356395

CONTENTS

ACKNOWLEDGMENTS

This book came about because a young man who once worked for my husband emailed me and asked if I would make a donation to a fundraiser his children's school was having. More specifically he asked if people could bid on being a character in one of my future books. I'd never done anything like that before, but I said certainly, knowing it was for a good cause.

As you read Murder and the Movie Star when you come across a character by the name of Roger Babowal, he is a real person and the father of my friend, Mike, and his sister, Shelly. Shelley was the high bidder at the school fundraiser and asked if, rather than using her as a character, I would use their father, Roger. I wrote and asked Mike if he could tell me something about his father. Once I began writing, Roger Babowal quickly became a very important character in the book, as you'll soon find out. So, thanks Mike, for asking me to do it and Shelley, thanks for submitting the high bid!

I would be remiss if I didn't thank Vivek and Tom, without whom, my books would never see the light of day.

To Vivek: It's wonderful to have someone I can rely on to take care of the things that you're so good at, namely, designing beautiful book covers, handling the technical side of publishing my books, and always giving me sound guidance.

To Tom: Our home operates seamlessly because of you, and for that I thank you! I could never take care of all the things that need to be done around the house and also find time to write. You're a living testimony that role reversals can work, whatever the age! Who would have thought a man who was once an important California State Senator would be doing the laundry and loading the dishwasher? Not me!

And To You, My Readers: Your ongoing support of me and my writing makes it worth every minute I spend doing what I love. Thank you!

Win **FREE** Paperbacks every week!

Go to www.dianneharman.com/freepaperback.html and get your FREE copies of Dianne's books and favorite recipes immediately by signing up for her newsletter.

Once you've signed up for her newsletter you're eligible to win three paperbacks. One lucky winner is picked every week. Hurry before the offer ends!

PROLOGUE

Jacquie Morton walked over to a painting hanging on the wall of her dining room that concealed a wall safe hidden behind it. Using her fingers, she felt the edges of the painting and carefully took it down. She couldn't see the numbers on the dial of the safe, but she'd memorized how many clicks she had to make each way to open it. When it swung open she reached inside and took out the large diamond necklace and rings she'd planned to wear tomorrow, the day of the big meeting, as well as the rest of her jewelry. With a gun pushed firmly into her back, she handed all of it, along with several large bundles of cash, to the person holding the gun.

The director of Jacquie's yet to be filmed movie, The Triangle, in which she had the leading role, was flying in from Los Angeles and meeting with her, the screenwriter, and the supporting actress, Lisette Andrews, in the morning to smooth out some differences they were having over the script. Now she wondered if she would even be alive for the meeting.

The meeting had been called by the screenwriter who was at a loss trying to understand why he was on the receiving end of negative and sarcastic remarks from Jacquie regarding the script he was rewriting for the movie. The director and the producer felt the movie could be in the running for an academy award in several categories, but they'd agreed the script needed some work. They knew they were taking a risk when they'd decided to make a film about the relationship between two women who were vying for the attention of the same man.

Jacquie was playing the role of a very wealthy older woman who was interested in a much younger man. Lisette was playing the part of a younger woman who was also vying for his attention. The movie was relying on clever dialogue and psychological nuances, rather than action, to make it appeal to the viewing audience. For that to happen, the script had to be perfect.

Jacquie had insisted that Lisette and Mickey, the screenwriter, come to Cedar Bay and stay in the house she owned next door to the one where she lived when she wasn't actively involved in filming a movie. She'd bought the house on a cliff overlooking the Pacific Ocean several years earlier as a retreat from the hectic life she led as one of the most famous movie stars in Hollywood. That was before she'd received the doctor's diagnosis three years ago that the eyesight problems she was beginning to experience were caused by the onset of macular degeneration.

Only her doctors in Beverly Hills and Cedar Bay, and her administrative assistant, Maizie Ortiz, knew how far the disease had progressed. She could still see shapes, but often she was no longer capable of determining who a face belonged to or reading the words on a script, which was why she'd opened the front door of her home a few minutes earlier. The person at the door had called her by name, and she didn't want the person to know she couldn't tell who it was by looking through the window pane in the door.

During the last two years, she'd come to rely on Maizie to be her eyes, particularly when she had to learn the lines in the rewritten script, so she'd be ready to meet with Mickey and Lisette the following day. She knew Mickey was frustrated by her response to his script, but she couldn't let either of them know that she simply couldn't read it. Instead of telling them about her vision disability, she made excuses by saying she didn't have the time to read the script, or whatever she could think of at the moment.

When Maizie had gotten the call that her granddaughter had to have an emergency appendectomy operation, Jacquie had told her to take a couple of days off and go to nearby Portland so she could be with her family. Even though the big meeting was to be held at her house tomorrow, it wasn't scheduled to start until 10:00, so she'd arranged for Kelly Reynolds of Kelly's Koffee Shop to bring several kinds of breakfast things to the house before the meeting. Maizie had gotten the coffee ready for Jacquie and arranged the cups, glasses, forks, napkins, and plates on the mahogany sideboard in the dining room. All Jacquie had to do was plug in the coffeepot, take the pitcher of orange juice out of the refrigerator, and set it out for her guests. No one would know what a struggle it was for Jacquie to make sure she could even do that, given her failing eyesight.

Her main concern was her makeup and hair, but as many times as she'd had to look "camera ready" over the years, she was sure she could do it from memory. Maizie had laid out the clothes she'd wear for the meeting, a dark pink silk pantsuit which accented her creamy complexion and thick, wavy, ash-blond hair. Looking at her piercing blue eyes, no one would ever suspect she suffered from a disease that rendered her nearly blind, a disease she'd managed to hide so far.

"Jacquie, it's me. Open up. I want to talk to you," the voice she recognized said. She'd opened the door and let the person in. She never saw the gun in the person's hand. All she felt was her arm being held in a tight grip, as the person walked her into the dining room where the wall safe was and demanded that she open it. When the safe had been emptied, the person propelled her towards the back of the house and opened the sliding glass door, letting in the sound of the waves breaking on the rocks below the cliff.

"What are you doing?" she screamed as she felt herself being pushed forward and the cold muzzle of the gun shoved into the middle of her back. She knew there was no point in struggling or trying to run for help, because she wouldn't be able to see where she was going. The one thing she realized with a sense of horror was that the person behind her was pushing her towards the sound of the ocean, towards the edge of the cliff.

"Your time here is over, Jacquie. You had a good run, but now you're through. Sorry to do this, honest. It's just the way things turned out."

With that Jacquie felt herself flying off into space. She screamed as loud as she could. She never saw the jagged rocks below that broke her back when she smashed into them, severing her spine. Fortunately for Jacquie, the force of the fall was enough to kill her instantly, and there was no pain or suffering.

Jacquie Morton, one of the most famous movie stars in the world, was lying dead at the bottom of the cliff. The only sound that could be heard was the rhythm of the waves breaking over the rocks, but Jacquie never heard them or saw them as her sightless, and now dead, eyes stared up at the dark sky.

The person standing at the top of the cliff knew time was critical, hurriedly walked back through the house, and began throwing the jewelry and cash into a small plastic bag. With that job finished, the person hurried to the front door. Within minutes, the house was empty and quiet. There were no witnesses and the person who had just murdered the famous movie star, Jacquie Morton, felt completely confident that the perfect crime had just been committed.

CHAPTER ONE

It was Monday morning, and the regulars were eager to begin their week with breakfast and coffee at Kelly's Koffee Shop, the gossip hub of the small town of Cedar Bay, Oregon. People often commented that if it didn't get talked about at Kelly's, it probably wasn't worth talking about. Kelly Reynolds, the genial owner, greeted each of them warmly and the words, "Would you like the usual today?" were often heard.

It had been a busy morning and as lunchtime approached Kelly went into the kitchen to see how her line cook, Charlie, was doing. "You need a break, Charlie? It's been pretty busy this morning, and I thought you might like to step outside for a minute and soak up the sun."

He grinned at her and said, "Ordinarily I'd take you up on that, Kelly, but I've got a great view of the coffee shop and guess who just walked in?"

Kelly was quiet for a moment listening to the unusual sound of silence in the coffee shop. She walked over to where Charlie was standing, and said, "Oh, my gosh, it looks like the rumors are true. I'd heard that Jacquie Morton had bought a home in that new area north of here that overlooks the bay, but I've never seen her. She's even more beautiful in person than she is in her movies." She watched as the head of every person in the coffee shop turned towards Jacquie, who graced them with her larger-than-life sparkling movie star smile.

"I think I've seen every one of her pictures," Charlie said. "Jacquie Morton is my all-time very favorite movie star. I wonder what she's doing here?"

"Having lunch, would be my guess," Kelly said. "Although I'm not sure Molly is going to make it to Ms. Morton's booth without falling apart. Look at her face. She's wearing the most idiotic smile I've ever seen." They stood there for several moments, watching Molly, the coffee shop's cashier and hostess, carefully hand a menu to Jacquie and the two people who were with her.

"Charlie, can you believe this? Look at Roxie. She's as star-struck as Molly seems to be. Now she's going over to their table to take their order. I can't hear what she's saying, but from the looks of it I guess she's asking them if they have any questions about the menu. As if the menu here has a lot of surprises on it. This is a coffee shop, for Pete's sake."

Just then the front door opened, and Kelly saw the familiar face of Doc Burkhart, a regular customer who had become a close friend of hers. He'd been the best man when she and Mike had gotten married a few years earlier. She watched as Doc walked over to the celebrity's table and smiled at Jacquie who smiled back at him. They exchanged a few words, and then Doc made his way to an empty table at the back of the coffee shop.

"Well, I better get out there before my help completely falls apart," Kelly said with a laugh. She delivered a couple of orders and then made her way to where Jacquie was sitting in a booth with a man and a woman. The woman looked vaguely familiar, but Kelly couldn't place her.

"Welcome to Kelly's Koffee Shop, Ms. Morton. I'm Kelly Reynolds, the owner, and I'm delighted to have you here. Will you be in town for long?"

"I don't think so. We're just taking care of some details in the script for my next movie, The Triangle. This is Mickey Sloan, the screenwriter. He's here trying to fix the original script he wrote," she said nodding in the direction of the handsome man with a full head of red hair and a matching beard. Kelly noticed the look of anger that passed quickly over his face. Jacquie continued, seemingly oblivious to his angry look, "And this is Lisette Andrews, the woman who has the supporting role in the movie. Naturally, I will star in it."

Kelly was shocked by the way she'd introduced the other two people, and although each of them was now wearing a pasted-on smile, neither of them seemed very happy with the introduction. "It's nice to meet you. I hope you enjoy your lunch, and if you have any questions, please feel free to ask."

"As a matter of fact, I do," Jacquie said. "I know Doc Burkhart, and he speaks very highly of you. I'm having a breakfast meeting Wednesday morning with these two and the director of the movie who's flying up for it. Doc said you might be able to cater some coffee cake and a few other breakfast items for the meeting. It's scheduled for 10:00. I'll talk to you on the way out, but first I want to see if the food is as good as Doc says it is."

"Of course," Kelly said, inwardly seething at the implication the food at Kelly's wouldn't really be all that good. "In the meantime, I'll be thinking of things I could make for your meeting." She turned and walked over to where Doc was sitting.

CHAPTER TWO

"Good noon to you, Doc. I see that you're punctual as usual," Kelly said.

"It's not me, Kelly, it's my stomach. It starts calling out to me about 11:30 in the morning, and before I know it, I'm in my car and on my way here."

"Well, you know you're always welcome. I see you've met our guest celebrity. I'm not sure the rest of the people in here are going to get what they ordered, given the condition of Molly, Roxie, and even Charlie. They're giving a new meaning to the word starstruck."

"So I've noticed. This may be the first time I've ever been in here that Roxie hasn't brought me a cup of coffee and a menu within moments of my arrival. Can't say I blame her, though. Jacquie is definitely a movie star from the old school."

"I assume that means you're on a first name basis with her."

"Yeah, I see her professionally from time to time."

Kelly knew that was a closed subject. Doc never talked about his patients or what they were seeing him for. "I don't know whether to thank you for referring me to her or not. We briefly talked about me making some breakfast items for a meeting she's having regarding her new movie."

"She can be a little difficult at times," Doc said, "but I think that comes from having people idolize you for so long. I know she's getting ready to shoot a new movie and from what I've read, she really needs this to be a hit, because the last one she starred in was a bomb."

"It must be pretty hard to take when you've been at the top of the charts for years and then you fall flat on your face while the whole world's watching."

"It is," Doc said cryptically and then changed the subject. "Coffee looks good. Thanks," he said to Roxie who had just walked up to him.

"Sorry about bein' a little late with your coffee, Doc," Roxie said breathlessly as she set a cup of coffee and a menu in front of him. "Things are kind of crazy with Ms. Morton in here." She put her head down, lowered her voice, and said, "Have you seen that necklace she's wearing? I've never seen diamonds that big dangling from a gold chain. And that tote bag on the seat next to her? I was reading one of those fancy fashion magazines the other day when I was at the beauty shop, and I'm sure that bag is a Hermes Birkin bag. Do you have any idea what those bags cost?"

"No," Doc and Kelly said in unison.

"Oh, not much. Just around $100,000, that's all. Can you imagine spending that kind of money on a tote bag? It boggles the mind. You could buy a house around here with that kind of money. Anyway, Doc, what can I get you today?"

"I'm in the mood for a grilled cheese sandwich and the soup of the day. Tell Charlie to make it a double. He made one for me a couple of months ago, and it was the best one I've ever had. Every so often I get a craving for one of his double grilled cheese sandwiches, and today's one of those days."

"You got it, Doc, assuming Charlie can even cook at the moment. Last time I was in the kitchen he was so busy staring at Ms. Morton, the orders were backing up. May take a little longer than usual. Just bear with us."

"No problem, Roxie. Now Kelly, what are you thinking of making for Jacquie?"

"Haven't had much time to think about it, Doc, but off the top of my head I've got a great recipe for overnight French toast. I think she'd like that."

"I know I would. How about those coffee cake muffins you make? They're one of my favorites."

"Good idea, Doc. Let's see, I could also make a hash brown sausage casserole and a bowl of fresh fruit. You know, those Hollywood types are always watching their weight, so there'd be something for everyone. What do you think?"

"I think I'd like to be invited," he said grinning. The two of them continued to talk for a few minutes and shortly Roxie placed a bowl of soup and the double grilled cheese sandwich in front of him. "Gotta get back in the kitchen. Ms. Morton's order is almost up," Roxie said.

Doc looked up and said, "What did she order?"

"Kind of strange if you ask me. She ordered a brownie and asked that it be warmed up. Nothing else, but I guess when you're a big star like her you can do whatever you want."

Kelly happened to be looking at Doc when Roxie told him what Jacquie had ordered and saw an angry expression briefly cross his face. It happened so fast she wondered if she'd imagined it.

He smiled at Kelly and said, "If I don't get a chance to tell Charlie just how good this is, would you do it for me?"

"Of course, but right now I need to write up a menu proposal, so I'll have something to give Ms. Morton when she leaves. See you later."

Kelly went back in the storeroom where her desk was and quickly typed up the menu proposal as well as the catering fee for the breakfast on the computer she kept in the coffee shop. As she walked back into the dining room, she saw Jacquie and her two associates walking over to the cash register. Kelly hoped Molly would remember how to work it when they paid.

"Ms. Morton, I hope you enjoyed your lunch. I took the liberty of typing up a menu proposal and my fees for catering the breakfast. Here they are." She handed the piece of paper to Jacquie who stuck it in her tote bag without looking at it.

"Well, since I'm used to eating in the best places in the world, I wasn't expecting much when I came here, but I did like that brownie. As a matter of fact, when you cater the breakfast Wednesday morning, I'd also like you to bring some brownies along with the other breakfast items. The meeting is at 10:00, so I want you to be there at 9:00. I'll have my assistant, Maizie, set up the table and have everything ready for you when you arrive."

"Why don't you take a look at my proposed menu, and if you have any questions, I'll be happy to answer them."

"No, I'm sure it will be fine. See you Wednesday," she said as the three of them walked out to a large BMW SUV. As soon as the front door had closed, everyone in the coffee shop began to talk excitedly. It was amazing how many people finished their meals at the same time that particular day. Kelly was pretty sure all of them wanted to be able to tell everyone they knew that they'd sat next to or near the famous movie star, Jacquie Morton.

CHAPTER THREE

Kelly wasn't any different. She'd gone home in the afternoon after she'd closed the coffee shop and could hardly wait to tell Mike her exciting news. Fortunately, their dogs, Skyy, a German shepherd just coming out of the puppy stage, Lady, a yellow Lab Mike had given her before they were married, and Rebel, the big boxer she'd gotten several years ago from the wife of a deceased drug detective, signaled Mike's arrival when all three of them raced to the door leading to the garage. Whenever they did that, Kelly knew Mike would be walking through the door momentarily, and so he did.

"Hello, my love," the big burly greying county sheriff said as he put his arms around her. Even though they were middle-aged, they made an arresting looking couple. Kelly was tall and full-figured and had her dark hair pulled up in her signature bun with two turquoise and silver hair picks.

"I hope your day was as wonderful as mine was," she responded

Mike pushed her back to an arm's length. "Wonderful? That's a word I'm not sure I've heard you ever use when you talk about the coffee shop. What happened that was so wonderful?"

"Before I tell you, why don't you change clothes, take off that gun, and when you come back, I'll have a glass of your favorite chardonnay, Rombauer, waiting for you."

"Consider it done," he said as he walked down the hall followed by the three dogs. It hadn't escaped the dogs' attention that Mike had opened the dog cookie jar on his way out of the kitchen. They knew the sound of the lid being removed from the jar meant they'd soon be getting a treat.

When he returned a few minutes later, he looked much more relaxed. "Thanks," he said taking the glass of wine she offered him. "Is this one of those wines your daughter found out about in her wine classes?"

"It is," Kelly said. "She told me it was one of her favorites. Actually, she's really doing well in them, and the school where she's been taking the classes has asked her if she'd be interested in teaching a class on introduction to wine."

"Wow, what a compliment to her. I think she'd be great at it, plus, she'd have a chance to do something more than take care of the ranch, the kids, and Brad. I know she loved her job in Portland, and even knowing how much she loves living at my aunt's ranch in Calico Gold, I'm sure she misses having something that's just hers."

"Agreed. She's tried to make a wine connoisseur out of me, but I can't tell a hint of blueberry from the essence of raspberry," Kelly said. "She tells me I'm hopeless. The only thing I know is if I like it or not."

"Unfortunately, I agree with you, but I can tell you one thing, I definitely like this wine. I don't know the price, but from the look on your face, I'm guessing this will not be a staple in our refrigerator. Would I be right?"

"That you would be, but back to my exciting news. Guess who ate lunch at the coffee shop today?"

"From the way you're quivering, I'll take a long shot and say the President of the Unites States."

"Nope, but you're close. Just one of the most well-known movie stars in the world, that's all."

"I hate to poke a hole in your balloon, but I think I know who it was. Jacquie Morton."

"How did you know that?" Kelly asked, turning to him with a look of astonishment, while she continued to stir the pasta sauce she was preparing for dinner.

"I've met the Beverly Hills, California, police chief several times at different conferences and as a courtesy, often if a police chief knows that a high-profile person will be in someone's district for a period of time, they let them know about it, so they'll be prepared if there are any problems. He called me a couple of months ago to tell me Jacquie Morton had announced to the media she was spending some time at her home in Cedar Bay, Oregon, preparing for her new movie. She said that the screenwriter for the movie and the supporting actress would be staying in the house next to hers, so they could work out the details before they started filming."

"Mike, you never told me about that. That's the kind of thing that brings a little glamour to our small town. I would have had the attention of everybody at Kelly's if I'd shared that news."

"Sorry, it just never occurred to me there'd be any reason for you to know. From what I hear, she's pretty high maintenance, and since I didn't think she'd be eating at Kelly's Koffee Shop, I didn't think any more about it."

"Mike, not only did she visit, based on Doc's recommendation, she hired me to cater a working breakfast she's having this Wednesday morning. I gave her a proposed menu and the cost, and she never questioned either one. She told me to be there at 9:00 a.m. She didn't even look at the menu or the cost, which I thought was kind of odd, but I guess if you're a big star, that kind of thing is beneath you. Oh, she did ask me to bring brownies along with the other things. That's what she had to eat for lunch today."

"That's all she had? Doesn't sound all that healthy," Mike said.

"You're right, and maybe that's why Doc frowned when Roxie told him what she'd ordered."

"As much as Doc loves the hamburgers and onion rings we share occasionally, that sounds a bit hypocritical."

"Could be, but I'd swear he had an angry look on his face for a moment. Guess she's a patient of his."

"Did he say what she was seeing him for?"

"No, and I didn't ask. You know how ethical Doc is. He never talks about his patients, and I respect that, but something didn't seem right about it to me."

"Yeah, he is very ethical, and it really is none of our business. When we finish eating, I need to return Lem's call. I never realized how seriously he'd take the job as campaign manager for my re-election." He took the spaghetti bowl she handed him and put it on the plate in front of him. "This looks fabulous. Who wouldn't like an Italian salad, warm bread, and spaghetti with a terrific sauce? You know it's one of my favorites. Tell you what. I'll do the dishes when we finish eating, and you can go in and relax in front of the TV. I'll join you after I talk to Lem."

"Sounds like a good deal to me. Thanks, and tell Lem I said hi."

CHAPTER FOUR

Mike ended his call with Lem and walked back into the great room where Kelly was watching television with all three dogs asleep on their beds.

"Mike, you look worried. Did Lem tell you something that's causing it?" Kelly asked.

He sat down heavily in the chair next to her and was quiet for several moments. "Sorry to be so slow in answering you, sweetheart, but I was thinking. Lem's really getting worried about my election, and if he's concerned, that makes me concerned."

"What did he have to say. Give me more specifics."

"All right. You know my opponent in the upcoming election is Rich Monroe. He's the police chief down in Little Harbor. Lem says he has a good reputation, and he's been the police chief there for about fifteen years, but that's not what's worrying him."

"Okay, I'll bite. What's worrying him?"

"Two things. Evidently the guy comes from big lumber money, meaning his family has been in the Beaver County area for generations, and they own a large sawmill. They've sold off most of their timberland. Rich never wanted to be a part of the family business, and he chose to go into law enforcement, eventually becoming the police chief of Little Harbor."

"That all seems pretty normal. I don't see any problems there."

"Well, there are. Here's the first one. He comes from a family that's very wealthy, and they don't tolerate losers. In other words, they're willing to fund Rich's campaign with whatever it takes to beat me."

It was Kelly's turn to be quiet for a few moments. "Mike, a lot of politicians have tried to buy elections in the past, and it almost never works. You've been the sheriff of Beaver County for over ten years, and from the little I know about politics, it seems that the incumbent almost always wins. Would that be a fair assessment?"

"Yes, if money was the only thing I had to worry about, but it isn't."

"Why am I waiting for the other shoe to drop?"

"Because it's dropping in the form of his wife. She's the second thing that's causing me some concern. His wife, Leticia, is Mexican. Her maiden name is Garcia. She's stayed close to the Latino community in the area and is very highly regarded. The media refers to her as the first lady of the Beaver County Latinos. She's publicly vowed to bring in that vote for her husband, and as I'm sure you know, that's a very large group of voters."

"Yuck, that is definitely the other shoe dropping. How does Lem suggest you combat those two things?"

"He wants to focus on my ability to solve crimes…"

Kelly interrupted, "With a little help from me."

"Yes, that's true, but may I remind you I'm the one who is the sheriff of Beaver County, not you? May I also remind you that I'm the one running in the upcoming election as the incumbent, not you?"

"Message received, but you don't need to get so prickly about it."

"Sorry, I guess I was, but for the first time since I filed my papers to run for re-election, I'm concerned. Lem thinks I need to compare my track record for solving crimes against that of Chief Monroe. Lem hired a researcher to see if he could find out anything about the chief that we might be able to use in our campaign. He calls it opposition research and evidently every candidate does it, although I never have in the past. But then again, I never needed to, since I was pretty much a shoe-in. He's found out that there are several unsolved murder cases from five years back in Rich's department, plus a case where he made a quick arrest and then it turned out the guy was innocent. Lem wants me to really hammer him on those things, both in the brochures I'll be mailing out, as well as in the speeches and debates that are scheduled between the two of us in the next few weeks."

"That sounds like good advice, but I can still see that worried look on your face."

"I'm just hoping nothing happens between now and the election that could affect my perfect record for solving cases."

"Mike, I think you'll be fine in that area. Yes, we've had a couple of murders in our little town, but everything seems pretty quiet right now, and I can't believe anything will happen that will make that change. But if it does, I'll help you however I can."

"Thanks, Kelly. I would like you to attend a couple of speeches with me, because you're so well-known in the area. Couldn't hurt to have you with me. Let's just keep our fingers crossed that we don't have any big crimes in the near future. If that happens, I'd have to solve the crime in a hurry or my campaign could be in trouble. Just between you and me, I think I'm too old to find another line of work."

"I honestly think you're worrying needlessly. I mean, what could go wrong?"

"Ever hear of that old adage called Murphy's Law?" he asked.

"Kind of rings a bell, but I'm not sure I remember what it stands for."

"Let's hope it doesn't happen. It's an old saying that goes something like whatever can go wrong will go wrong."

"Great thought, Mike. Keep that in mind, and you will lose the election. Nothing is going to go wrong, and on that note, I need to go to bed. Five in the morning comes very early, not that you'd know, because I'm always so careful not to wake you when I leave the house for the coffee shop."

"And for that I thank you," he said. "Okay guys," he said as he stood up and walked over to the door. "All dogs outside for one last time tonight."

CHAPTER FIVE

Mickey Sloan, the screenwriter for Jacquie Morton's new movie, The Triangle, sat at the computer in the house where he was staying just north of Cedar Bay, Oregon. The house was perched on a high cliff that overlooked the Pacific Ocean. It was owned by Jacquie Morton and located next door to where she lived.

He looked out the open window at the whitecaps in the distance and paused for a moment, listening to the roar of the ocean as waves crashed against the rocks below. He compared it to his favorite surfing place in California, Huntington Beach, and marveled that the same ocean could have two such different sides to it. There were miles of sandy beach in Huntington Beach and paddling out to catch the waves was easy to do there. Here in Oregon there was no beach, and no one in their right mind would even think of surfing in the angry turbulent water he was looking at, especially with the waves crashing onto the huge rocks that made up the shoreline at the base of the cliff. There was no sandy beach here.

He tried to get back in the rhythm of rewriting the script for The Triangle, but wondered why he even bothered. It seemed to be an exercise in futility. No matter how many rewrites he did of a scene, Jacquie always found something wrong with them, and she'd never even given Mickey the courtesy of reading the script in front of him. She always said she didn't have time, and she'd read it later that night. The next day it was the same thing all over again, although she did seem to know her lines from the day before. He was sure she just didn't like the script, but the reason why she didn't like the script escaped him, and she'd never given him anything specific.

Privately, he thought the producer had picked the wrong person for the lead role. Mickey wasn't about to be the bearer of bad news and tell one of the leading female movie stars in the world that she was too old to play the part of a woman who could attract the romantic interest of a man in his early thirties. Lisette Andrews, who was younger, was far more believable in her role as the young woman the man was interested in, thus completing the triangle. Mickey thought Lisette would have been a far better choice to play the leading role that Jacquie was going to play. He knew the director, Teddy James, had wanted Lisette, who was his mistress, to have the starring role in the movie. But the money men funding the movie had insisted they wanted a big name like Jacquie Morton to star in it, even though her last movie had bombed at the box office.

They were hoping the failure of her last movie was due to something other than her, like the subject matter, the economy, or the turmoil that was taking place all over the world. Mickey thought they should take their heads out of the sand and admit that Jacquie was simply past her prime.

Mickey knew his career would be over if he expressed his doubts about Jacquie being unable to carry the movie, so his options were limited. The last two screen adaptations he'd done, based on bestselling novels, had also bombed. He was pretty much in the same boat that Jacquie was in. He really needed The Triangle to be a huge box office hit, so his own career wouldn't tank. He felt he was between a rock and a hard place, and it wasn't a good way to feel.

He knew what he'd written was the best screenplay he'd ever done, but it didn't seem good enough for her highness, Jacquie Morton, and he was concerned she was going to demand that another screenwriter be brought in to write the final script. If that happened it probably would mean the end of his screenwriting career, and he might as well start thinking about finding a new career.

As he sat despondently looking out at the ocean he became convinced the only way to resolve the problem facing him was to have another actress replace Jacquie, but he also knew that because of her ego, not to mention how much she needed this movie to be a hit, that wasn't going to happen. That left him with one option. It was up to him to make it happen.

He looked over at the house next door, Jacquie's house, and noticed it had been built a little closer to the cliff than the one he was occupying, maybe by thirty feet. Mickey idly wondered what the chances were that someone could become disoriented and walk out the back door, mistaking it for the front door. In Jacquie's case, if that happened, if she did mistakenly walk out of the house, maybe after a couple of glasses of wine at night or taking a sleeping pill, it wouldn't be much of a stretch to imagine her falling over the cliff to the rocks far below. And if that happened, her body would probably be swept out to sea, never to be found.

Mickey didn't believe in violence. He tried to live his life as did his idol, Mahatma Gandhi, by practicing non-violence. If he didn't like something, he simply took a path of non-violent resistance. He began to justify Jacquie Morton's death as necessary, but the rocks below the cliff would provide the violent end to her life, not Mickey Sloan.

CHAPTER SIX

Wednesday morning Kelly quietly got out of bed, so she wouldn't wake Mike. After she'd dressed, let the dogs out, and quickly drank a cup of coffee, she loaded the casserole, muffins, French toast, and the brownies into her minivan, planning to put them in the refrigerator at the coffee shop until it was time for her to go to Jacquie's. She'd prepared them the evening before, because she knew how easy it was to get tied up in the morning rush of taking care of customers at Kelly's. The only thing left for her to do before she went to Jacquie's was to prepare a bowl of fresh fruit, and she knew she could easily do that while she was at the coffee shop.

When she arrived at Kelly's Koffee Shop she saw Molly, Roxie, and Charlie standing by the front door, waiting for her. "To what do I owe the pleasure of all of you being here so early?" she asked as she unlocked the door.

Roxie answered for them. "We've been talking and think you should take one of us with you this morning when you go to Jacquie's home to cater the breakfast for her meeting. We could help you serve and clean up. You know, none of us have ever been in a movie star's home, and this may be our only chance."

"Hate to disappoint you, but since I'll be gone, I need all of you to be here at the coffee shop. I really don't like to leave it during business hours, but I'm making an exception in this case."

"Do you think she'll have mirrored rooms and animal skins on the floor like you see in those stars' homes they show in all those supermarket magazines?" Charlie asked.

"I have no idea. I promise I'll give you a full report when I get back, but right now we need to get ready for the early morning breakfast crowd. Their business is just as important to the coffee shop as hers is. Now let's get to work."

Twenty minutes before Kelly was going to leave for Jacquie's she cut up the fruit and arranged it on a plate. She walked out to where Molly was standing by the cash register and said, "Wish me luck. I'm off. I shouldn't be gone more than two hours. I can go back after we close today and get my dishes. Hold the fort down while I'm gone."

Rebel was getting older and liked to spend his days laying outside near the front door to the coffee shop. The regulars all knew him, and a lot of them gave him treats which he gratefully acknowledged by licking their hands. When Kelly started to walk towards her car he got up and walked behind her. "Rebel, I'm not going home. Go on back to the coffee shop." He stood by the minivan in an uncompromising manner. She knew that once he made his mind up about something there was no way she could physically move him.

Kelly looked at her watch and realized it was later than she thought. She knew she didn't have time to try and insist he go back to the coffee shop. "Okay, come on, but if the big movie star doesn't like dogs, you'll have to stay in the minivan." He eagerly hopped in, always ready for a ride.

A few minutes later they pulled into the circular driveway in front of the large wood and glass house Jacquie had specially designed and built to fit her needs. She also owned the house next to it which was a smaller version of her home. Kelly noticed a large limousine parked in the driveway of the house next door and assumed it was the director's. She figured he'd probably flown into Portland early that morning and then driven to Cedar Bay for the meeting. She let Rebel out of the minivan, and they walked up to the glass front door. Kelley could see the ocean by looking through the door and across the large living room which ran the full depth of the house. She rang the doorbell.

When no one answered it, she knocked, thinking that maybe the doorbell was broken. Again, there was no answer. Kelly looked at her watch to make sure she was there at the right time, and confirmed that she was.

"Come on, Rebel. Let's check the back yard. Maybe she's out there gardening or something. I know this is the right time and the right day. Anyway, kitchens are usually at the back of the house, and that's where we need to end up."

They walked around the house on a sidewalk that led to the back yard, and Kelly knocked on the sliding glass door at the back of the house, as she looked across the living room to where her minivan was parked. No one answered her knock. She had her hands covering the sides of her eyes, trying to peer inside the house, when she heard Rebel's bark followed by a low growl. She glanced over to where he was standing looking down the face of the cliff at the rocks below. She noticed that the guard hairs along his back were standing up, indicating he was angry or alarmed, which she thought was strange. Rebel had been with Kelly long enough for her to know that if he sensed something was wrong, there definitely was cause for his behavior, and she felt a sense of foreboding sweep over her.

She walked over and stood beside him, looking down at the rocks below. She gasped involuntarily. A woman's body was sprawled on one of the large jagged rocks, not moving. Kelly looked closely down at the body, and recognized Jacquie Morton's signature ash blond hairdo. Jacquie wasn't moving, and there was no doubt in Kelly's mind that she was dead.

Kelly put her hand on Rebel and pulled him back from the edge of the cliff, at the same time taking her phone out of the purse she'd slung over her shoulder when she'd gotten out of her minivan.

A moment later, she heard Mike's voice on the phone. "Hi, sweetheart, so how's the movie star's house?"

"Mike, she's…" Kelly's voice broke as she tried to keep her voice steady. "Mike, Jacquie's dead. She's on the rocks below the cliff, and she's not moving. Rebel found her."

"Get back in your minivan, Kelly, and wait for me," Mike said in a commanding voice. "I'll be there in a few minutes. Lock your doors. If she didn't slip and fall over the cliff, someone may have killed her. Keep Rebel with you."

A few minutes later she heard the sound of sirens, and then Mike and two of his deputies drove into the circular driveway. She opened the window as Mike ran over to her minivan.

"Kelly, are you all right?"

"Yes, I'm fine. I'm a little shaky, but I'll be okay now that you're here."

"Good. Sorry, but I'll need you show me where her body is."

"Okay," she said opening her door. Rebel jumped out and ran over to Mike. "Follow me," she said as she led the way along the side of the house to the cliff. "She's down there," Kelly said, pointing to Jacquie's body. She heard more sirens and moments later three paramedics joined them.

Mike turned to them and said, "Looks like there's a stairway leading down to the ocean. The body's down there. My men and I need to go down there to inspect the immediate area and photograph the body. When we're finished, I want you to get a gurney and bring the body up as best you can. If you don't think that will work, you might have to sling her body over your shoulder. Any of you think you can do that?"

One of the paramedics was a large man who obviously spent a lot of time working out. He looked at Mike and said, "No problem, sir. It'll be a lot easier if I bring her up that way. Those stairs don't look all that secure, and if we're trying to handle a gurney loaded with a body, it could be a disaster. I'll do it."

"Thanks, but I don't think it could be much more of a disaster than what it already is."

An hour later, after Mike and his deputies had finished their work, the big, muscular paramedic arrived at the top of the stairs with Jacquie Morton's body slung over his shoulder. The other two paramedics had gotten a gurney out of their ambulance and were waiting for him. They carefully laid Jacquie's body on it and covered it with a sheet.

A short time later the coroner's van pulled into the driveway. The jowly florid faced coroner, with considerable effort, moved his big belly that was resting on the steering wheel and lumbered out of the van.

"What you got for me, Mike?" he asked. "When you called, you said it was a high-profile case. Don't know of anyone in these parts that's high profile with the exception of me," he said laughing.

"Name Jacquie Morton ring a bell with you?" Mike asked, trying not to let his dislike of the coroner affect how he handled the case.

"Course. Everybody knows Jacquie Morton. Why you askin'?"

"The body under the sheet on the gurney is Jacquie Morton, that's why," Mike answered.

"You're kiddin' me, right?"

"No, I wish I was. Looks like she fell off the cliff. I assume you'll be doing an autopsy to determine if she died of natural causes or if foul play was involved."

"I sure will, but if there's no signs of foul play who's to know whether she fell off the cliff by herself or had a little help? But I guess that would be your job, Sheriff. Sure glad it ain't me runnin' for re-election and havin' to solve Jacquie Morton's murder, if that's what it turns out to be."

"You're right. If she was murdered, it's really going to put me in a tight spot," Mike said grimly. He turned to Kelly. "Can you drive yourself back to Kelly's, or do you want to go home? This can't have been easy for you. At some point you're going to have to give a statement concerning how you found Jacquie. I can have Brandon call you later, and you can do it over the phone."

"Thanks. I'm fine, Mike, but I need to get back to the coffee shop and tell the staff what's happened before they hear about it from someone else. You know how fast rumors travel in Cedar Bay."

"Okay, sweetheart. I'll probably be late for dinner tonight. I'll call and let you know once I get through the paperwork this is going to require. See you later." He hugged her and turned to his deputies. "Let's go inside. We need to find out who the next of kin are and notify them before the media finds out about it. This is going to be a high-profile nightmare for our department." He and his men entered the house through the unlocked back door, while Kelly and Rebel walked around the side of the house to her minivan.

CHAPTER SEVEN

As Jose Hernandez drove to Jacquie Morton's house to do his weekly gardening chores, he thought about what Serena, his wife, had told him the evening before about her doctor's visit. He still couldn't believe it. His world, as he knew it, had come to a crashing halt.

She'd told him the doctor had said she had a disease called ALS, and that most people knew it as Lou Gehrig's disease. The doctor said she was in the early stages of it, and that's why she'd been having cramps in her legs at night when she was in bed and beginning to have difficulty when she swallowed and talked.

Jose had said he'd never heard of it and asked what the doctor had told her she could do to get rid of it. She'd started to cry and said there was no cure, that she would just get progressively worse until she wouldn't be able to walk or talk and eventually would need a feeding tube. She was concerned how much longer she'd be able to work at her job as a bookkeeper for the insurance agency in Cedar Bay.

He didn't know what they were going to do. With three children, they needed the money from both of their salaries just to feed their family and have a roof over their heads. They'd gotten married right after they'd graduated from high school. Although their parents were illegal immigrants, Serena and Jose had both been born in the United States, and they were U.S. citizens. Their parents had returned to

Mexico a year after their wedding, because as they got older, they'd missed being with their extended families.

Serena had excelled in high school and soon after their marriage she'd started working for the Cedar Bay Insurance Agency. She loved what she did and from what her boss had told her, she was very good at it. When Serena would have to stop working because of ALS, the money she earned would stop as well, plus, who was going to take care of her when Jose was working?

Now that their families were in Mexico, there wouldn't be anyone able to help. Maybe Jose and his daughters would have to go to Mexico to live when she died, and from what his wife had told him last night, it was inevitable. He didn't know who else could help him raise their three daughters or how he'd find the money to even feed them. Jose's mind was a jumble of thoughts, and none of them were pleasant.

He parked in the circular driveway of Jacquie's home and took out the gardening equipment from the back of his truck. He cut the grass in the front yard, edged it, and started to walk down the brick pavers on the side of the house to do the back yard. When he finished mowing and edging the back yard, he wanted to plant the flowers Jacquie's assistant, Maizie Ortiz, had asked him to bring.

As he pushed the lawnmower along the side of the house he happened to glance through the window that looked into the dining room. He saw Ms. Morton and Maizie standing in front of what appeared to be a wall safe with a painting propped up against the wall underneath it. It looked like Maizie was taking jewelry out of the safe. Each time she took a piece out, she handed it to Jacquie, and she appeared to be describing it to her, which seemed very odd to Jose. He wondered why Ms. Morton didn't take the jewelry out herself and why Maizie would be describing the pieces to her. Surely Ms. Morton could tell everything about the pieces just by looking at them. He didn't understand what was going on.

The more he looked through the window, the more amazed he was at the sight in front of him. Along the sides and in the back of the safe he saw stack after stack of what appeared to be bundles of hundred dollar bills. He stared in astonishment for several minutes as Maizie continued to take jewelry out of the safe and hand it to Ms. Morton. In the short time that Jose watched the two women, he estimated that Maizie had taken twenty to thirty pieces of jewelry out of the safe. While he couldn't make each piece out, he noticed that several of the pieces appeared to be necklaces, and he imagined the smaller pieces were rings and bracelets.

Jose didn't want the two women to catch him staring through the window, so he made his way to the back yard and continued to mow and edge the lawn. When he was finished, he went back to his truck and took out a flat of dianthus and baby's breath flowers. He intended to plant them along the sides of the back yard. When he'd bought them he'd thought how well the pink hues of the dianthus and the white of the baby's breath would play against each other and the green lawn.

He was just finishing up when Maizie came outside. "Good morning, Jose," she said to the handsome dark-haired young man. "The flowers that you just planted are beautiful, and I'm sure they'll be even more so when they get a little larger."

"Thank you, Maizie. I hope Ms. Morton likes what I've done. You told me she wanted me to pick out some plants I thought would do well here on the coast, and I think these will look great when they fill out. Do you think she'll come out to look at them while I'm here?"

Maizie hesitated a moment, and then she said, "Jose, I don't want you to feel you've done a bad job or that she doesn't appreciate your work, but sometimes Ms. Morton has trouble seeing things. It's just a temporary condition, and although it's not public knowledge, I thought you should know. Please don't tell anyone."

"I didn't know that, and of course I won't say anything. Thanks for telling me, Maizie. I would have wondered why she didn't come out or say anything, particularly since you told me she was the one who wanted me to buy and plant them."

"Now you know, Jose. By the way, how are Serena and the children doing? Be sure and tell them hello for me. I still remember how wonderful her tamales were when you had me over for lunch."

He looked at her with a painful expression on his face.

"Jose, is something wrong with Serena or the girls?" she asked with a sense of dread.

He tried to tell her, but unbidden tears sprang into his eyes, and his voice became hoarse. He appeared to be on the verge of breaking down. After a few long moments, he got control of himself and told her what the doctor had related to Serena the day before regarding her condition, both the diagnosis and the prognosis.

Since Jose no longer had any family in the United States, Maizie had begun to think of him and treat him like a son. She looked at him with a horrified expression on her face and said, "What are you and Serena going to do?"

He was quiet for several more moments, and then he answered, "Honestly, I have no idea, Maizie. I never expected anything like this to happen, particularly not at our age. You know we don't have any relatives here, and there's no one who can help us. I don't know what to do."

"I come from a big family, Jose, and we always take care of our own. Even though most of my family lives in Southern California, some of them don't live far from Cedar Bay. When you get to the point where you need help, let me know, and I'll see what I can do."

"Thank you, Maizie. I'm sure things will work out, but right now I sure don't know how."

"None of us ever does, Jose. Sometimes we just have to trust there's a higher power helping us. I believe in that higher power, and you need to as well. I have to get back inside. Ms. Morton's daughter, Kim, is coming over in a little while. She called this morning and told her mother she wanted to talk to her. I want to make sure everything is ready for her. Do you mind if I tell Ms. Morton about Serena? I know how much she likes you."

"No, there's no reason to keep it a secret."

"I'll be praying for you and your family, Jose. I'll see you next week, and those flowers are beautiful. Thank you, again, and please tell Serena how sorry I am."

Jose finished up in the back yard, and as he was walking along the sidewalk to the front yard he thought of what he had seen being taken out of the wall safe and also the piles of cash that were in the safe.

If I had those jewels and that money it migh not keep Serena from dying, but it sure would solve a lot of my problems. I could hire someone to take care of her and even keep our family together here in the United States. I wonder what I'd have to do to get into that safe. Whatever it is, it would be worth it if it helped Serena, and Ms. Morton's so rich, she could afford to just buy more jewelry, and I doubt if she'd even miss the money.

On the drive to the next job on his route for that day he thought of how wonderful it would be if he could get the jewels and the money he'd seen. He finally came to the conclusion that even if something bad had to happen to Jacquie, if it meant Serena's time on earth was more comfortable, it would be worth it. He doubted the higher power Maizie talked about would approve, but a man had to do what a man had to do to take care of his family.

CHAPTER EIGHT

Kim Morton walked back to her small cabin after taking a shower in the communal bathhouse at the retreat center Guru Dev had built in the foothills near Cedar Bay.

She replayed in her mind the conversation she'd had with her mother, Jacquie Morton, the last time she'd visited her at her home. Kim had gone there to see if she would be willing to give Kim an advance on her inheritance, so she could help Guru Dev, but that hadn't worked out at all. Her mother had insisted she leave the retreat center and live with her in the home she owned in Cedar Bay. She told Kim if she didn't leave Guru Dev and the retreat center there was a good chance she'd cut her out of her will entirely, instead of giving her an advance on her inheritance.

Kim really didn't care about her mother's money, her status as a movie star, or even the perks that having a famous movie star for a mother had given her when she lived in Beverly Hills. She'd been told a number of times that she should get an agent, because with her perfect figure, flawless complexion, and natural ash blonde hair, she was stunningly beautiful and turned heads wherever she went.

Kim was always surprised when people told her how beautiful she was. How she looked or how others perceived her was completely unimportant to her. She was far more interested in living a private life and working on her inner spirituality, and for her that meant living at the retreat center and renouncing the earthly comforts her mother's success in life had afforded her.

Kim walked over to the large building where the morning devotionals were held, took her place on her meditation cushion, and closed her eyes. Usually she could clear her mind and achieve something close to the peace of mind Guru Dev spoke of in his weekly talks, but not this morning. Try as she might, her mind remained a jumble of thoughts, mainly about her mother.

She couldn't understand why her mother was being so selfish about her money. Kim was an only child, her mother was divorced, and from what she knew, her mother didn't have a romantic interest in anyone. It didn't seem fair for her to have that much money and not give some of it to Kim.

She and Guru Dev had talked many times about building more retreat centers. He was becoming increasingly popular, had developed a large following, and many of his followers wanted to make his retreat center their permanent home. As wonderful as it sounded, he didn't have the money to make it happen.

The young woman dressed in a loose white tunic and pants, which all of the devotees at the retreat center wore, who was sitting next to Guru Dev, rang a small bell indicating that the morning devotional had ended. Kim felt a hand on her shoulder and looked up into the smiling face of Guru Dev.

"Kim, I would like to talk to you. Please come to my quarters."

She stood up and followed him to the small cabin where he lived. It was the dwelling of an ascetic, someone who had renounced most earthly things. There were only two rooms plus a bathroom. In one room, there was a large bookcase filled with spiritual writings, a sound system for the chants he liked to listen to when he was doing his daily yoga practice, a yoga mat, and a black zafu, or meditation cushion, which looked like it had been used a lot.

In the second room was a single bed with a sheet and a blanket.

There was no bedspread or pillow. The only other piece of furniture in the room was a table Guru Dev had made into an altar with pictures of his guru, as well as a string of the mala beads he used when he was meditating. Fresh flowers and lit candles were also on the altar. He lived a spartan life and ate his meals with the others in the communal dining hall.

He handed a second zafu to Kim and indicated she was to sit on it while they talked. "So, tell me, my child, how did the talk go with your mother?" he asked.

She looked into his large kind brown eyes and said, "Not well, Guru Dev. She doesn't really have a spiritual side, and doesn't understand why I'm living here, rather than with her. She told me when I reject her lifestyle it's as if she's had a slap in the face from me. The movie star," Kim said bitterly, "is a very difficult, self-centered woman. She's used to getting her way, and as a matter of fact, she made a veiled threat that if I didn't leave your retreat center and live with her, she would disinherit me."

"I am so sorry, my child. I don't know where else to turn. Although I've increased my fees when I conduct meditation or yoga groups, they still are not enough to pay for the new retreat centers we've dreamed and talked about. Do you think it would help if I talked with your mother?"

"No. She thinks anything to do with yoga or meditation is ridiculous, and I would never put you in a position where you had to defend what you believe in and teach. I wouldn't submit you to that. Give me a few more days. I'll try and think of something."

"Thank you, my child. Right now, your mother is my only hope. I have several students who have means, and they have offered to help me, but I need more than they have offered to pay me in order to build the centers. I still want you to work with me when we do build them. I have great faith that they will be built. We just need to find a way to do it."

He stood up, the white robe and turban he always wore accenting his olive complexion. Guru Dev smiled at her, "Don't worry, child. We will make this happen."

As she walked back to her cabin, Kim's mind was churning. Her mother had made it very clear to her she was not going to give Kim an early inheritance, and she was certain if Guru Dev ever tried to set up a meeting with her, it would be a disaster. It seemed the only way she could give Guru Dev the money he needed was if she inherited it, and for that to happen, her mother, the famous movie star, Jacquie Morton, would have to be dead.

As much as Kim didn't like what she was thinking, it might be the only thing that would work. It went against all of her spiritual training, but she remembered reading something once about the ends justifying the means. Maybe this was one of those times. She wasn't happy with her decision, but she didn't see an alternative.

CHAPTER NINE

Every time Deke Cannon got ready to go to work at the restaurant where he was a waiter he got angry all over again thinking about the way his life had turned out. He'd had it all for a while. Deke was the starting quarterback for one of the most prestigious professional football teams on the West Coast, and he was married to Jacquie Morton, one of, if not the, most highly paid movie stars in Hollywood. The fact that she was also extremely beautiful had been an added plus. His life was split between football practices, games, and red carpet entrances to important events with Jacquie by his side.

The press called them the perfect family. Although Jacquie had a daughter, Kim, who had been born out of wedlock, she'd never revealed the identity of the man who had fathered her child. Rumor had it that even Kim didn't know who her biological father was. Kim was seven when Deke and Jacquie got married. Kim had adored her stepfather, and Deke felt the same way about her. For several years, it had been an idyllic existence, then things began to fall apart.

Deke was in the Super Bowl, getting ready to throw a pass to his wide receiver and never saw the sack coming. Unfortunately, his body was in an unnatural position as he looked around for his receiver, and the crushing violent tackle by the three hundred-fifty-pound defensive lineman took him completely by surprise. When he woke up several hours later he found himself in a hospital room surrounded by nurses, doctors, his agent, and several members of his team. The doctor had asked everyone to leave the room. He didn't want them to be there when he told Deke he would never play football again, and he was certain the star pro football player wasn't going to take it well. The doctor had told Deke his leg had been broken in several places, and his hip had been shattered. He'd said Deke would be in the hospital for several weeks and then transferred to a rehabilitation center that specialized in helping people who needed to relearn how to walk.

When Jacquie had been told, she'd flown in from Italy where she was filming a new movie and blithely assured him that if he couldn't play football anymore it was no big deal, she'd help him find work in the movie industry, and so she did. With Deke's rugged good looks, muscular physique, and deep blue eyes, everyone was sure he'd be the next big star. What no one had even considered was whether or not Deke could act. He couldn't, and it was very apparent to everyone, including Deke, after he'd been in three movies, that any thoughts he'd had of having acting as a second career, much less being a star, were totally unfounded.

Jacquie was at the height of her career and didn't have the time or the desire to support a husband whose life was pretty much over when he was just thirty-two. She'd told him what a loser he was, and she was sorry she'd ever married him. She divorced him and never looked back. Because of his well-known name, his agent had been able get parts for him in several porn movies, but as much as he would have liked the money, that wasn't how he wanted to be remembered, and he told his agent he wouldn't act in porn movies.

He remembered all the letters he'd gotten from young men who were football fans of his, and he was sure their parents would not approve of their son's idol going into that profession. His agent had told Deke that was as good as he was going to get, considering how he'd bombed out of the legitimate movie industry because of his bad acting. He explained to Deke that if he wouldn't take those roles, he couldn't do anything more for him, and he would no longer be Deke's agent.

A few days earlier, Deke had been in a supermarket buying groceries when he'd seen a picture of Jacquie on the cover of a celebrity gossip newspaper. While he waited in the checkout line he'd idly leafed through it and read the interview a reporter had done with her. He was stunned to see where she'd said that she'd made a huge mistake when she married Deke, because he turned out to be such a loser.

The article said she'd laughed when she was told by the reporter that he was considering working as a waiter, because that was about the only job he could get. She'd even hinted he'd taken the restaurant job hoping to catch the eye of some producer or director, and they'd give him a chance to try and make another movie. She'd said if they did, it would be a disaster, because some people just couldn't act, and it was very apparent to anyone who had seen him try, that he was one of them.

The tabloid article ate at him over the next few days, and every time he thought about it, he became furious all over again. In one of his angry moods he remembered how much Jacquie had loved her jewelry. He remembered telling her early in their relationship that her jewelry took a back seat to her beauty. Deke winced, remembering it. Several times before they were to attend some important event she'd had him open her safe to get certain pieces out when she was running late

He knew Jacquie was a creature of habit, and Deke was willing to bet she still used the same combination to the wall safe she probably had at her home in Cedar Bay as the one she'd had in her home in Beverly Hills. He idly wondered how she'd feel if all of her jewelry mysteriously disappeared. That might cause her some grief, and no one would ever suspect him because he lived in Southern California. He'd read that she was spending a few months at her home in Oregon, the house Kim had told him about. He figured he could sneak into the house when she was asleep, or perhaps she might even let him in. He could play it by ear and see what happened. Who knew, Jacquie might even have to have a bad accident. The possibilities were endless.

Deke smiled for the first time in several days, but it was a very cold calculating smile. His young football fans would never associate that smile with the smile the papers had always referred to as his game face smile.

CHAPTER TEN

The afternoon at Kelly's Koffee Shop had been particularly hectic when word had gotten out that the well-known movie star who had a home in Cedar Bay had fallen to her death from the cliff outside her home. It was the type of story that had everything – glamour, mystery, and the possibility of murder. When something like that happened, everyone wanted to talk about it, and Kelly's was always the place the local residents came to do just that. Somebody there might have news, and no one wanted to be the last to know.

It was later than usual when Kelly and Rebel finally left the coffee shop. She hurried home to let Lady and Skyy out in the back yard. Although Kelly and Mike had put a doggie door in the garage, so the dogs could get out in the back yard when they needed to, she still felt better when she'd actually seen them go outside.

She checked the crock pot chili she'd started that morning and turned it down to low, not sure when Mike would be able to get home. She was curious what the media had to say about Jacquie's death and went into the office she and Mike shared to begin her search. Jacquie's death was all over Twitter and Facebook. References were made to everything anyone could come up with about Jacquie Morton. Kelly had planned on doing a Google search on Jacquie to see what she could find out, but given all the information available on those two sites, she figured it would just be needless repetition.

People were talking about Jacquie's new movie, her last movie that had bombed, her ex-husband, and her daughter, although not much was known about her. Cedar Bay was prominent in the discussions and even though not too many people had known where it was, Jacquie's death had certainly put it on the map. Kelly thought the next day might be one of the busiest days the coffee shop had ever had, because she was certain that along with the regulars, there would probably be a lot of media people who would be traveling to Cedar Bay to cover the entertainment industry's biggest story of the year. All those out-of-town visitors were going to need to eat. The few hotels and motels in the area always recommended Kelly's Koffee Shop to their guests, so it was a safe bet that tomorrow would be a very busy day at the coffee shop.

When she heard the dogs rushing to the door leading to the garage, Kelly knew Mike was home. She walked out of the office and opened it for him. "Well, Sheriff, how bad was the rest of your day?" she asked.

"I've had better. Give me five minutes to change. I'll meet you in the kitchen, and yes, you could get me a glass of wine."

"I don't remember asking," she said grinning.

"It was unspoken. You know me well enough by now to know that the day a possible murder happens, I can definitely justify a glass of wine before dinner."

Five minutes later she handed him a glass of the Rombauer that had been left over from the night before. "Glad you agree that the day also calls for one of my favorites, even if it does cost a little more than what we usually have on hand." He sat down at the kitchen table and took a sip of his wine. "Ahh, nectar of the gods."

Kelly sat down across from him. "What's happening with the Jacquie Morton case? Did you find out anything?"

"The coroner said his preliminary examination didn't show anything that would point to her being murdered, but he's having a number of tests run, so it's probably going to take a couple of days to get the results."

"It could have been a case of her simply becoming disoriented, losing her balance, and falling off the cliff," Kelly said.

"I would agree with you except for one little thing."

"And that one little thing being..."

"The wall safe was wide open and empty. There was a painting on the floor below it leaning against the wall, so I assume the painting usually covered up the wall safe. That speaks of both robbery and murder to me. We have no idea what was in the safe, and her administrative assistant, who might know what was in the safe, is gone for a couple of days.

"There was a note from her giving Jacquie instructions for her meals. I thought it was kind of interesting that the note was written in really big printed block letters. I have no idea what that means. Her gardener came to work today and mentioned that the granddaughter of Jacquie's assistant had to have an emergency appendectomy, and she was going to be with her daughter and her family in Portland for two days. She's supposed to be back shortly."

"So, if it does turn out to be a murder investigation, you always tell me to start with who has the most to gain when someone is murdered. When I was on the Internet before you got home, I read that she had a daughter, Kim, but not much was known about her. Her name is Kim, and I assume she will probably have the most to gain if she inherits her mother's substantial estate."

"That's true, and I had to call her and tell her about her mother's death. Juan, the gardener, was the one who told me Jacquie had a daughter who lives near here. I found her phone number on Jacquie's cell phone contact list. Like you said, the daughter's name is Kim, and she lives at that retreat center a couple of miles from here. If you remember, we drove by it one time. It's run by some Indian guru, and people come from all over the country to study with him."

"What was her daughter's response?" Kelly asked.

"Not quite what I would have expected. I asked her if she had any idea what had happened, and if she knew of anyone who could possibly be involved if it was determined that foul play was involved." He stopped talking and took a sip of his wine. "What was interesting was her response."

"Why?"

"She didn't seem all that broken up. I asked her what her relationship was with her mother, and she said they were somewhat estranged, because Jacquie wanted her to leave the retreat center and live with her. She said her mother didn't approve of Guru Dev, yoga, or meditation. Then she went on to say that her mother was a very difficult person to be around, and if foul play was involved, she wouldn't be all that surprised."

"Wow. That's kind of a cold response when you hear that your mother was found dead."

"I thought so, too. I asked her if she knew what had been in the wall safe, and she told me that her mother kept a large amount of cash and her jewelry in it. My next question was who would have access to it."

"I'd be curious about that as well," Kelly said.

"Her answer was interesting. She said there were several people who knew the combination, and she was one. Kim said her mother's assistant, Maizie Ortiz, knew it, and she was pretty sure Jacquie's ex-husband, Deke Cannon, knew it as well. She said there may have been others, but she couldn't think of any more."

"So, what are you going to do with that information?"

"Remember when I told you that I knew the Beverly Hills police chief? I'm going to call him and see if he knows anything about the ex-husband. My secretary told me Jacquie had recently given an interview to some celebrity gossip magazine, and there was a scathing reference in it to Deke, her ex-husband. I called Jacquie's attorney, and he said even though Jacquie and Kim were not on the best of terms, Kim will inherit her entire estate, which he said was pretty substantial. He said as soon as Maizie Ortiz returns from her granddaughter's surgery, he'll have her inventory what's in the house, so he can begin to probate the estate."

"Well, if this turns out to be a murder investigation, there's your first two suspects," Kelly said. "I wonder if there are any others."

"I don't know. When I talk to my friend, I'll ask him if there's anyone in the movie industry who might qualify as one. He's pretty wired to it, so maybe he can help."

Just then Mike's cell phone rang. He pulled it out of his pocket and answered it. "Hi, Lem, no, Kelly and I were just sitting here talking. What's up?" Mike listened to him for several minutes, and Kelly noticed that Mike had a very concerned expression on his face.

"Rich said that? Seriously? The woman hasn't even been dead one day, and he has no idea if she was even murdered." He listened to Lem and then said, "Lem, don't worry. He's just blowing smoke, trying to create headlines. If she was murdered, I'll solve the case. I promise you it will not affect my re-election, no matter what he says. I'll call you tomorrow after I know a little more." He ended the call and looked grimly at Kelly.

"I gather your opponent is already making noises about the Jacquie Morton case," she said.

"Yes. He's thrown down the gauntlet and said if it was his case, he'd solve it in hours. Rick also said if I can't solve it within a few days, it's just proof that this county needs a new sheriff, and he's the one who should be elected."

"Well, Sheriff, in that case, I guess we need to determine once and for all if Jacquie Morton was murdered, and if she was, then we have to solve the murder and catch the killer."

Mike raised an eyebrow and said, "No, not we, Kelly. I need to solve this case. I don't want you to get involved in it. You inadvertently were involved this morning by being in the wrong place at the wrong time when you discovered Jacquie Morton's body, but that's the extent of it. Do we have an understanding?"

"Of course, Mike. It was just a slip of the tongue."

"I'm going to believe that it was, because I would hate to think that you would deliberately get involved in something when I've specifically told you that it doesn't involve you."

"Consider it done, Sheriff. Now it's time for dinner."

CHAPTER ELEVEN

Lisette Andrews picked up her cell phone and called Teddy James, the man who would be directing The Triangle. The call was immediately answered, and she heard Teddy warmly say, "Darling, how are you this morning? I'll be so glad when you begin filming down here. I'm lonely without you."

"Me too, Teddy. I'm cold, and it's overcast here half the time. I need to get back to Southern California and soak up some sunshine."

"Just a couple more weeks, and Mickey should have that script the way Jacquie wants it. How are things going on that end?" he asked.

"That's why I called, Teddy. It's not going well at all. I'm beginning to wonder if there's something wrong with Jacquie. I know she has a reputation for being a real diva, but the way she's been acting lately goes way beyond what you might expect from a diva. I really feel sorry for Mickey. She disses whatever he writes, although she never reads anything in front of us. Jacquie says she concentrates better when she's alone at night. Several times Mickey has asked her to read a page or two when the three of us are together, and she's refused. I wonder if she has some physical problem. The whole thing seems very strange to me, because after she bombed in her last film, she really needs this one to be a hit, and I'd think she'd want to do whatever is needed in order to get back on top."

Teddy was quiet for several long moments and then said, "I just wish I'd been able to get the financial backers of The Triangle to see that you were the one who was absolutely perfect for the lead. Jacquie's too old for it, and I'm worried this film is going to bomb like her last one. If it does, that's going to affect both of our careers. Let me make a couple of calls and see if I can find out anything."

"Thanks, love, I miss you. When are you coming up here?"

"I'll be there in a few days. Jacquie's asked for a meeting with you, Mickey, me, and the producer, Lou Jordan. We decided on next Wednesday, so it won't be all that long, and I can't wait to see you."

"Me, too, baby," Lisette said. "See you then."

After Teddy ended the call, he sat at his desk thinking what he should do. His reputation was on the line, and he was very concerned about Jacquie's behavior. The last few times he'd seen her he thought something was off about her, but he couldn't put his finger on it. He knew she'd had what she called "maintenance work" done over the years by the plastic surgeon he'd sent all of the studio's starlets to. Maybe he'd know what was going on with Jacquie.

A moment later a receptionist answered his call, "Dr. Trumbull's office. How may I direct your call?"

"This is Teddy James. I'd like to speak with Dr. Trumbull. Would you tell him I'm on the line? Thank you." He was pretty sure Roy would take his call, if for no other reason than Teddy had sent him a lot of patients over the years and was probably responsible for Roy being able to afford the large yacht that had been prominently featured on the Christmas card Roy sent out last year.

"What a surprise, Teddy. I never hear from you, but you keep sending me all those beautiful women who work for you. What can I do for you?"

"I'd like your professional opinion regarding one of your patients," Teddy said.

"Happy to help if I can, but I'm sure I don't need to remind you of my oath involving patient-physician confidentiality."

"Of course not, Roy, I'm well aware of it. Just as I'm aware of how much all the women I've sent you contributed to the new boat that you featured on last year's Christmas card. I'm sure those referrals allowed you to buy it."

There was silence on the other end of the line for a few moments and then Roy asked, "What would you like to know, Teddy?"

"Thanks, Roy. I knew you'd see it my way. I want to know if there's anything going on with Jacquie Morton. I know she goes to your office several times a year for botox treatments and a little nip and tuck here and there. She seems off to me, like something's wrong with her. My reputation and a lot of money are riding on her new movie, and if there's a problem, I need to know about it."

Again, it was quiet on the doctor's end of the line. Teddy heard him take a deep breath and say, "Teddy, there is a problem. About three years ago Jacquie was in here for a couple of treatments, and I thought she was having problems with her eyesight. I gave her the customary consent form to read and sign, and she said she'd read it later. I told her I needed her to read it and sign it before I could administer the treatments to her. She broke down and told me she'd been having problems with her eyesight and that her assistant, Maizie, had become her driver and essentially her eyes."

"Oh no, I was afraid of something like this." Teddy said. "No wonder she won't read the script in front of the screenwriter. Sounds like she can't. I'm assuming you referred her to someone who's an expert in that area."

"Of course I did. Dr. Magnussen called me back a few days later and told me that Jacquie Morton was in the early stages of an eye disease called macular degeneration. I'd heard of the term, but I wasn't all that familiar with it, so I asked him what the prognosis was."

"What did he say?" Teddy asked, thinking that a movie and his career was riding on what he was going to hear from the doctor in the next few minutes.

"He said it was incurable, and it would only get worse. It doesn't result in death, but it often results in the patient becoming blind or very close to it. I'm sorry, Teddy. I'm sure that presents a problem for anyone trying to read a script."

"That it does, Roy, that it does."

"Teddy, I'd appreciate it if you didn't use my name if you tell anyone about this. My giving you this information is highly unethical. If you don't mind my asking, what do you intend to do about this situation?"

"I don't know, Roy. I need to think about it. Obviously, it needs to be handled very delicately, but I certainly don't see how Jacquie can star in a movie if she can't even read her lines."

"I'm sure you'll come up with a solution, Teddy. I have to go. I'm due in surgery in a few minutes. See you at the premiere."

After the call ended, Teddy continued to sit at his desk, deep in thought. He wondered how he would ever be able to extricate himself from the mess he was in. Finally, after an hour spent thinking of all the different alternatives, he made what he considered to be the only decision he could make. Jacquie Morton could not and would not star in The Triangle, and he would do whatever it took to make sure she didn't. A plan began to form in his mind, and for the first time since the movie's backers had insisted Jacquie Morton play the lead, he felt confident the movie could be a hit, but a few things had to be taken care of, like Jacquie Morton, for one.

CHAPTER TWELVE

The next morning Kelly turned off the alarm clock before it could go off and wake Mike. She knew when he was involved in a case he needed all the sleep he could get. She took care of the dogs, made a cup of coffee, got dressed, and she and Rebel left for the day. She quietly closed the front door, and then the two of them headed out to her minivan which she'd left in the driveway the previous afternoon.

She normally never picked up the morning paper which was always on their sidewalk when she left for the coffee shop each day, since she knew Mike loved to read the cartoons, and he'd told her he always went out and got the paper as soon as he was up, even before he poured himself a cup of coffee. For some reason this morning she bent down to see what the headline was and gasped when she read it. There, on the front page above the fold, was a picture of Mike with the headline "WILL THE DEATH OF JACQUIE MORTON, THE BELOVED MOVIE STAR, MEAN CURTAINS FOR SHERIFF MIKE REYNOLDS?"

Kelly picked the paper up and quickly scanned the article. It was all about Jacquie's death and how Mike's opponent, Police Chief Rich Monroe, said if Sheriff Mike Reynolds couldn't find out how Jacquie had died, it was just one more reason that the county needed a new sheriff. Kelly's first instinct was to hide the paper from Mike, but she knew if he didn't read the article while he was at home, he'd buy a newspaper on the way to the station, or there would even be one waiting on his desk for him when he got there. She thought that the timing and the way Jacquie had died couldn't have come at a worse time. For the first time since Mike had decided to run for re-election, she was concerned his campaign might not be successful.

When she got to Kelly's Koffee Shop, she knew her prediction that the day would be especially busy because of Jacquie's death had been absolutely correct. There were several cars already parked in front of the coffee shop, waiting for it to open. Molly, Roxie, and Charlie were already there as well. She greeted them, unlocked the door, and started the big commercial coffee urn, knowing she could at least give her customers a cup of coffee while they waited for Kelly and her staff to do what was necessary to get the coffee shop operational.

"Kelly, I'm sorry about the article the newspaper ran about Mike and his opponent. What did Mike say about it?" Roxie asked.

"I don't know. The paper was on the sidewalk when I walked out to get in my minivan. I usually never pick it up, but for some reason this morning I did. After I read it, I took it back in the house for Mike to read. I debated taking it with me, so he wouldn't see it, but I knew he'd either buy a newspaper or there would be one at the station. Someone would make sure he read the article, but it didn't sound like very objective reporting to me. Mike's opponent, Rich Monroe, has started to run a very nasty campaign and with a few more weeks left before the election, I wonder what other dirt and unfounded claims he'll make. The only saving grace is that Mike and I lead pretty boring lives."

"Yeah," Roxie said. "The next thing you'll know there will probably be a picture of Rebel, Skyy, and Lady, along with some of the dogs you helped rescue when Maggie Ryan was murdered and they found over thirty dogs in her house. I can see it now. The headline will read something like 'Sheriff Reynolds and Wife Break County Law by Owning More Than Three Dogs'. And it will probably be above the fold. After this morning's article, who knows what that guy will come up with?"

"Thanks, Roxie. That makes me feel even better," Kelly said sarcastically.

"Sorry, but I'm just so angry about that article. Mike has to be the best sheriff this county has ever had, and it infuriates me that some sleazy chief of police who happens to be running against Mike is trying to discredit him. Actually, I'm surprised the paper even published it."

"I know, Roxie, I felt the same way when I saw it. I wish there was something I could do to help Mike, but right now I'm not sure what it would be."

"Kelly, you'll think of something. You always do. Mike's lucky to have you watching his back. I predict you'll find out what happened to Jacquie, and Mike will easily win his campaign for re-election."

"I appreciate your confidence and, believe me, I hope you're right. Those are predictions I like, but now we need to get this coffee shop open and ready for business. Look at the line that's already formed at the front door. This may be the busiest morning we've ever had. I hope we don't run out of food."

Roxie turned around, looked at the door, and shook her head. "I recognize some of the people, but there's a lot of faces I don't know. Think it's people who are here because of Jacquie's death?"

"Sure do, and with that, it's time to open for business. Ready, Charlie?"

He smiled from his place in the kitchen and gave her a thumbs-up. "Don't worry, Kelly. I've got the cooking fairy on my shoulder this morning, and she's going to make sure everyone leaves here fat and happy."

She grinned at her staff. "Thanks, guys. I really don't know what I'd do without you. Okay, it's show time." Kelly unlocked the front door and within minutes almost every seat in the coffee shop was occupied. Roxie and Molly delivered menus and coffee to the customers, and tried to keep everyone happy as best they could.

The morning went by in a blur. None of the staff had a moment to sit down, to say nothing of Charlie's normal cigarette break which he took in the morning whenever there was a slow time. Not only was every seat taken in the coffee shop, there were always people standing by the door, waiting for customers to finish eating and relinquish their seats.

Promptly at noon, the coffee shop door opened, and Doc Burkhart walked in. His usual smile was gone and in its place, he wore a somber expression. When Kelly'd noticed his truck drive into the coffee shop parking lot, she'd taken a seat at a small table, waiting for him to come in. She waved to Doc, and he walked over to the table.

"Thought I better save this one for you, Doc. Seats are at a premium today. Why such a somber look?"

"I've been thinking about Jacquie Morton's death all night. Kelly, I spent a little time researching this, and I learned that once a patient dies, the confidentiality part of a patient-physician's relationship dies with them." He looked at her expectantly as if he thought she'd understand what he was saying.

"Doc, I'm afraid you've lost me. I have no idea what you're talking about."

"I have some information I think Mike needs to know about Jacquie Morton. She was my patient, and as I just said, confidentiality is no longer an issue. As you know, my wife Liz is a psychologist, and she was treating Jacquie Morton as well. Last night we talked for a long time and decided we both need to talk to Mike. Any chance we could come by tonight after we get off work?"

"Doc, I know he'd want to talk to both of you, particularly if you think you have some information about her that Mike should know, but here's the thing. He's giving a speech to the Veterans of Foreign Wars this evening around 7:30. Any chance you could come by the house about 5:30?"

"We'll find a way to make it happen, Kelly, even if we have to reschedule a couple of appointments. I think what we have to say is important and relative to the investigation concerning her. We have a feeling she didn't fall down that cliff on her own."

"Doc, are you saying you think she was murdered?" Kelly asked incredulously. Until now she really hadn't thought it was a possibility.

"I don't know, that's Mike's area of expertise, but what we both have to tell him may shed a little light on it. He can process the information we give him and decide what, if anything, to do with it."

"Thanks, Doc. After that newspaper article this morning, I think he can use all the help he can get."

"I agree, and that's partly why we decided to come forward sooner rather than later. It was a sleazy article, and I'm surprised the paper even printed it. It was really unfair and biased, and I would have expected a lot more from the editor. He's a patient of mine, and I intend to tell him exactly how I feel the next time he comes to the clinic."

"Doc, I don't want to tell you your business, but may I suggest that maybe politics and medicine don't mix."

"You can suggest it, but I also have to live with myself, and I really can't until I say something to him. Don't worry about it. It's my decision, not yours."

"Your call, Doc. See you and Liz about 5:30, and Doc, thanks."

"What are friends for?" he asked waving Roxie over to give her his order.

CHAPTER THIRTEEN

The afternoon at Kelly's Koffee Shop was just as busy as the morning had been, and when it was time to close for the day, Kelly and her three employees felt like they'd definitely earned a little time to wind down from the day. She waved goodbye to them, locked the door, and she and Rebel walked over to where she'd parked her minivan early that morning.

She didn't know why, but for some reason she felt she needed to go to Jacquie's house. A few minutes later she found herself driving north to where the house was located high on a cliff overlooking the ocean. She parked in the circular driveway and noticed that yellow tape had been draped around the house, indicating that it was an area where a crime scene investigation was being conducted. Kelly had no desire to go inside the house, but she wanted to see if she'd missed something on the outside.

Kelly and Rebel circled the house, noticing that the house next door was almost identical to Jacquie's, but smaller. She remembered Mike had mentioned something about Jacquie owning the house next to hers and renting it out to the man who was doing the screenwriting for her upcoming movie as well as the actress who was also in the movie, the two who had been with Jacquie at the coffee shop.

When she and Rebel got to the back yard, she saw a tall man with thinning black hair who was holding a leash attached to the collar of a Brittany spaniel behind the house on the other side of Jacquie's house. A small woman who was wearing glasses was standing next to the two of them. Kelly noticed that the woman was wearing an auburn colored St. John knit suit which perfectly matched her thick shoulder length hairstyle. They were looking at a large ship far out on the ocean. As Kelly and Rebel started to make their way to the trio, the woman walked to the driveway, got in a car, waved to the man, and drove away.

Kelly walked over to the man and the dog and said, "Hi, my name's Kelly Reynolds. This is Rebel, and trust me, he's very friendly." Rebel walked over to the man's dog and gently sniffed the orange and white well-groomed dog.

"Pleased to meet you, Mrs. Reynolds. My name's Roger Babowal, and this is my dog, Rusty. You probably saw my wife, Chris. She's the one who just drove away. She's meeting a visiting professor who's come to town to pick her brain. It happens all the time. She used to teach linguistics before she retired, and she was pretty well thought of in her field."

"Mr. Babowal…"

"Name's Roger. How about if I call you Kelly, and we'll dispense with being formal? Chris and I live here," he said, motioning to the house next door to Jacquie's. "So, what brings you out here on a nice day like today?"

"Roger, my husband, Mike, is the sheriff of Beaver County. I'm sure you know that your next-door neighbor, the movie star Jacquie Morton, was found dead at the bottom of the cliff over there. I help my husband from time to time on his cases, and I was wondering if you heard anything or noticed anything night before last, the night she died."

He ran his hand over his oval face, took a sip from a glass of what looked like iced tea, and stared out at the ocean. Finally, he turned to her and said, "Yeah, I heard a woman screaming that night. She wasn't screaming anything in particular, just screaming, but it was sort of a terrified scream if you know what I mean, and then it just stopped. I've been wondering ever since I heard that Jacquie Morton had died if the scream I'd heard had come from her."

"I suppose we'll never know, and I also suppose she would have screamed whether she'd accidentally fallen over the cliff or someone had pushed her over the edge."

"I have no idea, Kelly, but I've been thinking about it a lot. When you live next door to someone you kind of expect you'd get to know them, but she never spoke to me or to Chris. Several times we saw her outside, but it was almost as if she couldn't see us. Maybe she was someone who valued her privacy so much she didn't want to acknowledge her next-door neighbors."

"Roger, I only met her once, so I have no idea. Is there anything else you can tell me? Did you ever hear any unusual sounds coming from the house, like arguments, or things of that nature?"

He was quiet, seemingly lost in thought. "Kelly, I have kids, and there have been a few times over the years when my children and I haven't agreed on certain things. Several days ago I heard an argument between a young woman I'd seen go into Jacquie's house earlier. I'm pretty sure it was her daughter, because when they were arguing I heard her use the word 'Mom,' and she looked like a younger version of Jacquie Morton. I couldn't help but notice someone that beautiful.

"Sometimes I still like a cigarette, and I come outside when Chris is watching television or has gone to sleep. She gets pretty bent out of shape about my smoking. I've decided it's one of those things a spouse is better off not knowing. Anyway, I was out here having a smoke when I heard the argument."

"Can you tell what it was about?"

"I caught a few of the words, and it seemed like Jacquie was telling her daughter she didn't want her living at some place anymore.

She said the guy was a fake, and that she wanted her daughter to move in with her. Her daughter sounded really angry and said whoever it was they were talking about was not a fake, and she would never move back in with her mother, because she didn't want anything to do with her or her lifestyle. I remember that part pretty clearly because her daughter slammed the front door, and I saw her pull away in her car and speed down the road, but I don't know what that would have to do with her death." He stopped and took another sip of his iced tea.

"Nor do I, Roger, but thanks for telling me. Mike's told me many times that when he gets a lot of little pieces of information, it leads to bigger ones, and it's sort of like when a tipping point happens, and then the case gets solved. Maybe what you've told me will help him. I'm sure you won't mind if I tell him. Can you think of anything else?"

"Of course I don't mind if you tell him. Happy to do it. There is one other thing, and it's only because it bothered me at the time. Ms. Morton's gardener comes every week, and as soon as he finishes the front yard, he takes his equipment around to the rear of the house and does the back yard, then he leaves. When he was here last week, he stopped on the sidewalk on his way to the back yard and looked inside the house at something for about five minutes. It didn't sit well with me. I wouldn't want my gardener kind of spying into my house, if you know what I mean."

"I agree. That does sound unusual. I wonder what he was looking at," Kelly said.

"I have no idea, but I suppose any odd behavior has to be looked at when a death has occurred. Anyway, if I can be of help, let me know. Been nice talking to you and tell your husband good luck. If there's been some foul play, sure hope he finds out who did it, since my home is next to the one where the woman died."

CHAPTER FOURTEEN

Promptly at 5:30 Doc and Liz arrived at Kelly and Mike's house with their dogs, Max, a bulldog puppy that was the latest addition to the Burkhart family, and Lucky, the yellow Lab Kelly had given Doc after they'd become friends.

Kelly raised an eyebrow and said, "Doc, are you taking both dogs into the clinic these days?"

"No, my last patient of the day cancelled, so I went home and got Lucky. Until I get to the point where I can trust Max not to get into anything, I'll keep taking him to the clinic every day. I have a wire kennel I keep him in when he's there. Hope you don't mind, but I thought they'd like to play with your dogs."

"I'm sure my dogs will be thrilled you brought them. I'll open the sliding door and let them out," she said as she walked over and opened it. A few minutes later all five dogs were running back and forth in the back yard, thoroughly enjoying their time together. After a couple of minutes had gone by, Rebel, the oldest of the group and definitely the alpha dog, decided he'd had enough and laid down on the grass watching the antics of the younger ones, particularly Skyy and Max, who were exhibiting all the traits of energetic young puppies.

"Okay, now that they've been taken care of," Kelly said, "how about some lemonade? I made a pitcher when I got home, and thanks to perfect timing, Mike's car just pulled into the driveway."

They both nodded that lemonade would be great, and a moment later Mike walked in. "Hi Liz, Doc," he said as he kissed her on the cheek and shook Doc's hand. "Kelly called me and told me you were coming over. I'd really appreciate anything you can tell me about Jacquie Morton, because quite frankly, this case is driving me nuts. The opponent in my race for re-election is making her death the central point of his campaign, so I can use all the help you can give me."

"Let's go sit down in the great room," Liz said. "We can keep an eye on the dogs while we talk. I don't anticipate any problems, but with five dogs I like to err on the side of caution."

When they were all sitting down with their lemonades in hand, Doc said, "You know Liz and I never talk about our patients, but since Jacquie Morton is dead, we did a little research and we're not violating the oaths we took by talking to you now that she's deceased. Quite frankly, both of us have some concerns that she didn't fall down the cliff on her own."

"What are you saying, Doc? Do you think she was the victim of foul play?" Mike asked.

"That's your area, Mike, but let me tell you what I know, and then Liz can tell you what she knows, and maybe it will help you solve the mysterious circumstances surrounding her death." He took a sip of his lemonade and said, "Jacquie called the clinic when she came here a couple of months ago, and asked to speak with me. When I took her call, she wanted to know if I was familiar with a disease called macular degeneration."

"I've never heard of it," Kelly said. "What is it?"

"It's an eye disease that occurs when the small central portion of the retina degenerates. It causes eyesight problems and as the disease progresses, makes it difficult for the person to read or even identify things. Everything becomes quite blurred."

"I've heard of it," Mike said. "I remember something about it being age related."

"That's true," Doc said. "It generally happens to people when they're older. Anyway, I told Jacquie I'd treated people for it in my practice when I was in Southern California, and I actually have two patients here in Cedar Bay I'm treating for it. I won't bore you with the details, but people who have it are often prescribed a medication known as anti-VEGF medication which blocks the vascular endothelial growth factor, thus the name of the drug. I know that's pretty technical stuff, but I just wanted you to know I've had some experience with the condition. Jacquie told me she was being treated for it in Southern California and made an appointment to come in and see me."

"I'm going to interrupt, Doc," Kelly said, "but if she was having problems with her eyesight, that might account for her never acknowledging her neighbor." She looked over at Mike and said, "I had a long talk with him today, and he told me she'd never talked to him."

"She probably couldn't see him," Doc said. "She told me she was really concerned about her upcoming movie, I think it's called The Triangle, because she couldn't read the script. She said she'd made a lot of excuses to the screenwriter about why she wouldn't read his revisions when he gave them to her. She told me her assistant, Maizie, had become her eyes. Evidently Maizie would read the script to her, and Jacquie would try to memorize her lines. She said it was really difficult, and she thought the screenwriter was getting very angry with her. I told her I thought she needed to see Liz, because it sounded like she was having some psychological issues as well."

"I'll take it from there, Doc," Liz said. "Jacquie came to see me once a week after Doc recommended that she do so. I probably saw her about seven times, and I have to tell you that there were a number of things that concerned her. First of all, she and her daughter had become somewhat estranged. Her daughter had chosen to live in the The Loving Care Retreat Center not too far from Cedar Bay. The guy who heads it is from India, and I believe his name is Guru Dev. Jacquie felt he was a quack, and she thought the only reason he'd befriended Kim was to get money from Jacquie. From what she told me, she and her daughter had fought bitterly about it."

"Her neighbor heard Jacquie and her daughter arguing about it, too, and he told me her daughter left the house really angry," Kelly said.

"That doesn't surprise me, but there were other things that bothered Jacquie. She really regretted marrying Deke Connors, the pro football player who blew out his leg and hip. He's the one who couldn't play football anymore and tried an acting career, based on Jacquie's recommendation. She said she took it personally that he was such a lousy actor, and when she'd heard he'd been offered some parts in porn movies, it had been a total embarrassment to her. She told me he was constantly calling her asking for money, because he was broke and the only legitimate job he could find was working as a waiter. She also mentioned she'd given an interview to a gossip tabloid about what a loser he was, and he'd become furious with her for having done that."

"I'll second the lousy actor thing," Mike said. "I thought the guy was a great football player, so when I heard he'd become an actor I checked out one of his movies. It was horrible. Hands down, he was one of the worst actors I've ever seen."

"Liz, what other problems did she have?" Kelly asked.

"She was really concerned that her career was over, and she was exhibiting all the signs of someone who's suffering from depression. She knew the producer and financial backers of The Triangle wanted her to have the starring role in the movie. Jacquie told me the director, a man by the name of Teddy James, was romantically involved with the supporting actress, Lisette Andrews, and had wanted her to have the lead rather than Jacquie, but as I just said, the film's backers had insisted on Jacquie having the starring role. She didn't know how she was going to be able to make the movie with her diminishing eyesight. She was afraid someone would find out about it and use it as a reason to release her from the movie, and she knew if that happened, no one in Hollywood would ever again ask her to be in a movie."

"Wow, poor thing. That's a lot to worry about along with having your eyesight getting worse and worse."

"Yes," Liz said. "Doc didn't mention that one of the things he'd recommended to her that helped slow down the disease is eating well-balanced meals. He told me how angry he'd been to find out that all Jacquie had eaten when she was at your coffee shop for lunch was a brownie."

"Doc, I thought you looked angry for a second, but it happened so fast, I never asked you about it," Kelly said.

"Guess it doesn't matter now," Doc said.

"Anyway," Liz continued, "I asked Doc to give her a prescription for Xanax, because I thought she was getting more anxious by the week, and I thought it would also help with her symptoms of depression. I knew it wouldn't solve her problems, but it might help her deal with them in a less emotional manner. That's about all I thought you should know. Doc, do you have anything to add?" Liz asked.

"No," he said turning to Mike. "I don't know if any of this helps your investigation into her death, but we thought you ought to know. If foul play was involved, seems to me there are a few people who would have had a motive, but that's your department, not mine. Kelly told me you have a political speech you have to give tonight, so we better gather up the dogs and head on out. Kelly, see you tomorrow at lunch."

A few minutes later, after Doc, Liz, and their dogs were gone, Kelly and Mike got in his car to go to the Veterans of Foreign Wars building across town.

"Well, Mike, what do you think? Did you find anything they had to say useful?"

"All of it, but I just don't know what I'm going to do with it."

"I want to see that retreat center where Jacquie's daughter is living," Kelly said. "Roger Babowal mentioned the argument he heard between Jacquie and her daughter, and that seemed to be at the heart of it. I also thought I'd go back to Jacquie's house tomorrow after I close Kelly's. Maybe her assistant has returned, and she might know something that would be of help."

"Kelly, normally I'd ask you not to do either of those two things, but given what I'm dealing with, I probably could use your input. Just be careful."

"Thanks for that rare vote of confidence in my abilities, and I really mean it. What's on your agenda for tomorrow?"

"I need to call my friend, the Beverly Hills police chief I mentioned to you. I'd like him to find out everything he can about Deke Cannon, and what the rumors are about the film Jacquie was going to be in and all of the people connected with it. If it's determined that she was murdered, at least I can say we're investigating several people of interest."

"Maybe by this time tomorrow we'll know something definite."

"I sure hope so," Mike said, "because if we don't, I may be flipping hamburgers at the local fast food burger joint pretty soon."

"I'm going to pretend I didn't even hear that," Kelly said.

CHAPTER FIFTEEN

The parking lot of the Veterans of Foreign Wars was almost full when Kelly and Mike arrived and they had a hard time finding a place to park. Kelly didn't know if that was a bad thing or a good thing. On one hand, she hoped everyone had come to hear Mike give a speech, but a small little voice in the back of her head said maybe it was because of Jacquie Morton's death and what Mike's opponent, Rich Monroe, was probably going to have to say about it.

They walked into the building and were immediately greeted by a distinguished looking older man wearing a white uniform shirt, a cap, and American flag shoulder patches. "Sheriff Reynolds, all of us here at the VFW are looking forward to hearing from you. My name's Scott Nichols, and I'm the Post Commander." He shook Mike's hand and turned to Kelly. "You must be Mrs. Reynolds. Thank you for coming tonight."

"Thanks for having us," Mike said. "Where would you like us to sit?"

"Sheriff, you'll be up on the stage with Rich Monroe. I'll be in between both of you, and I'll introduce you. Mrs. Reynolds, I reserved a seat for you in the front row. I trust that's all right."

"That's fine, thank you," she said.

"Sheriff, Mrs. Reynolds, I'd like to introduce you to some of our members before we get started. I expect Chief Monroe to be here shortly, and we'll get started as soon as he arrives. As you may have noticed, a number of our members are a little older and don't like to stay up too late, so we try to start our meetings promptly."

The next twenty minutes were spent in introductions, shaking hands, and what's commonly called in politics, 'working the room.' They heard a commotion at the door and saw Chief Monroe enter with two of his uniformed deputies. Scott Nichols walked over to the chief, greeted him, then walked back to where Mike was standing. "Chief Monroe is here. Let's get started. You can sit in the chair on the right side of the stage."

"Good luck, sweetheart," Kelly said to Mike as he turned and walked up the steps to the stage. She took her seat and watched Chief Monroe walk up on the stage and shake Mike's hand.

"Please, everyone, take a seat," the Post Commander said. "We're about to hear from the two candidates in the upcoming election for Beaver County Sheriff. When they've finished giving their talks, we'll have our usual business meeting, but I didn't want to be the one responsible for these lawmen being tired tomorrow. Who knows how many bad guys they'll have to catch, and I didn't want to be the one responsible for either of them missing a bad guy." Everyone laughed.

The Post Commander introduced Chief Monroe who stood up and walked over to the microphone. "Thank you for giving me this opportunity to speak to you. I won't bore you with my accomplishments or those of my department. They're well documented on the flyer that my deputies are passing out. I simply want to tell you several things. I am committed to winning this election, because it's time for a change in Beaver County. Quite frankly, we need a new sheriff.

"The reason I'm running is for the same reason that nothing is happening in the Jacquie Morton death case. Do we know if she was murdered? No. Do we know if it was the result of natural causes? No. Let me tell you one thing. If she was murdered, and I happen to think she was, none of us is safe from harm, because there is a murderer at large in our county. Does that make you feel you elected the right man to be sheriff in the last election? I certainly hope not, because my family and I sure don't feel safe right now, and we won't until the murderer is caught.

"I pledge to you if I was your county sheriff, I would be doing everything in my power to find out whether or not a murder has been committed. I certainly wouldn't be attending a Veterans of Foreign Wars meeting to talk about an upcoming election. That election pales in the face of a possible murder."

He turned and faced Mike. "Mr. Reynolds, can you, with certainty, tell the people here tonight that they are safe, and that a murderer isn't on the loose in our county?"

Kelly knew Mike well enough to know how angry he was, but she also knew she was probably the only one to spot the signs. She had no idea how he was going to handle this ugly attack on his ability to carry out his job as the sheriff of Beaver County.

Mike walked over to the podium and looked out at the audience. The room was quiet, waiting for his response. "Ladies and gentlemen, thank you for giving me the opportunity to speak to you, and Chief Monroe, thank you for bringing up what's on the mind of everyone here. Was Jacquie Monroe murdered or did she die from an inadvertent fall over the cliff? That is the question on everyone's mind, and none more so than mine, but while I have thought about nothing else since her death was discovered, I also have an obligation not to rush into making a judgment that could mean an innocent person is charged with something he or she did not do. That's happened before in our county, and I don't want to see it ever happen again."

It was an obvious reference to when Chief Monroe had arrested a young man for raping a schoolgirl, only to find out that the girl and several of her friends had concocted a false story to get back at the young man who had refused to attend a Sadie Hawkins Day dance with her. The chief looked at Mike and glowered at him.

Mike continued to speak. "My department and I feel confident we will soon be able to make a determination about what happened to Jacquie Morton, but rest assured, when we do, an innocent person will not be arrested. By the way, so we don't waste the taxpayer's money, the men in my department are working on this case as we speak, rather than passing out election brochures for me. Let me get back to the subject of Jacquie Morton's death. If it was an accident that resulted in a fatal fall, that is a tragedy, and simply one of those unexplainable things that sometimes happen to good people.

"However, if her death is determined to be a homicide, I promise that the guilty party will be arrested immediately. My department already has created a list of several persons of interest, and we are looking into their whereabouts on the night she died. Believe me, we are leaving nothing to chance, but we certainly will never act in a rash manner just to make headlines. I wish I could stay and talk with you at length. I even considered cancelling tonight's talk, given the events of yesterday, but I felt I owed it to you to tell you personally that each and every one of you can go to sleep tonight knowing your sheriff is doing what you elected me to do, and that's make determinations based on fact, not attention-grabbing headlines. Again, thank you for inviting me to speak with you this evening."

He concluded his talk and came down the steps, nodding to Kelly who stood up and joined him, as they walked over to the door and out to their car. They heard footsteps behind them and then a voice said, "Sheriff, can you spare a minute? I have something I'd like to tell you."

They turned and saw a man who looked to be in his sixties walking towards them. "Yes, what is it?" Mike asked.

"Sheriff, I've been an admirer of yours for a long time, and I think you're a very fair and honest man. If you find out that Jacquie Morton was murdered, you might want to take a look at her ex-husband, Deke Cannon, and here's why. My son served in the Army with Deke, and not many people know that Deke was given a dishonorable discharge. People never think that about a football hero, but there was talk he'd killed some innocent villagers during his tour in Afghanistan.

"Although the Army couldn't prosecute him for it, because they couldn't prove it, they did give him a dishonorable discharge. Just thought you might not know about it, because his publicity people were very careful to see that it was kept out of the media and never saw the light of day. Everyone knew when he went into the Army that he was going to play pro ball when he was discharged, so they wanted to keep his reputation as lily white as possible."

"Thank you, sir, I didn't know that. My department is looking at everyone who had a connection to Jacquie Morton, and as a matter of fact, I'm going to have the police chief in Beverly Hills check out Deke. When I talk to him, I'll see if he knows anything about the dishonorable discharge. I really appreciate you telling me about it."

"Happy if I could be of service. Good luck in the campaign, but if what I saw in that room tonight is any indication, I wouldn't worry. You'll be a shoe-in."

"Wish I shared your optimism my friend, but thanks. I appreciate it."

When they were in the car, and the man had walked back into the Veterans of Foreign Wars building, Kelly turned to Mike and said, "You gave a brilliant speech. It was a perfect response to what that horrible man was insinuating. I'd be willing to bet you have the respect and vote of everyone who was in the room."

"Smoke and mirrors, babe. If I can't solve this within a couple of days, that speech won't be worth the paper I wrote it on, and I know it will come back to haunt me in the days leading up to the election. I have to find out if Jacquie Morton was murdered and if she was, who did it."

"You will, Mike, don't worry. You will." In her mind, she changed the word 'you' to 'we,' but felt it might be a good thing to keep it to herself as her own little secret. She spent the rest of the drive home figuring out how she was going to help Mike, the man she loved and adored, and who obviously had a tough political fight on his hands, which had been ratcheted up several notches because of the death of Jacquie Morton.

CHAPTER SIXTEEN

The following morning when he got to the station, the first thing Mike did was call his friend, the chief of police in Beverly Hills, Ron Jacobs. A few minutes later Mike heard him say, "Mike, I can't say this call is unexpected. I assume it's regarding Jacquie Morton. Would I be right?"

"That you would be, Ron. I have a couple of favors to ask of you."

"Shoot. I'll see what I can do."

"I'd like to know what you can tell me about Deke Cannon, her ex-husband, as well as the rumors on the street about her new movie, The Triangle. Anything you can tell me about the people associated with it would be very helpful to me, and if you know anything about her daughter, Kim Morton, I'd like information on her as well."

"Let me see what I can find out. When do you want it?" he asked.

"Like yesterday. You see, Ron, here's the deal. I'm running for re-election as the sheriff of Beaver County, and I've got an opponent who is really making a big deal out of Jacquie Morton's death. Plus, the local residents are getting nervous, and I can't say I blame them. The coroner is still running some tests, but so far, we don't have anything that specifically indicates she was murdered. There were no signs of foul play on her body, but it's hard for me to believe she walked that far out of her house, in the dark, and then just stepped off the edge of a cliff and fell to her death. Something I haven't mentioned is that her wall safe was cleaned out. Doesn't pass the smell test, if you know what I mean."

"I do, and I'll see what I can come up with. Why don't you give me your cell number? I can probably get back to you with something in a couple of hours."

"Thanks, Ron. I'm not sure how I'll be ever be able to return the favor, but try and think of something."

"That's not going to be a problem. What I'm thinking is that Oregon has some pretty good rivers for trout fishing, and I know you're a fisherman as am I. Might ask you for a little help in that area," he said laughing

"Consider it done whenever you want, and Ron, thanks. I knew I was going to owe you, and that's okay." He ended the call, thankful that at least it felt like something was being done on the case.

Mike was going over some reports of work his deputies had just completed when his cell phone rang two hours later. He recognized the area code as that of Beverly Hills. "Ron, I'm hoping this means you found out something," Mike said.

"Actually, I found out quite a bit. I started with Deke Cannon. He's working as a waiter in an Italian restaurant in Beverly Hills. Rumor has it that he hopes to be discovered again by an agent or someone in the business. I had one of my men call the restaurant manager, and he confirmed that Deke was working on the night Jacquie Morton died. He was at the restaurant until it closed at midnight. I believe you told me the coroner estimates Jacquie died around ten or so in the evening. I think that effectively eliminates him as a suspect, although we did turn up something about him that I've never seen in print."

"What was that?" Mike asked.

"There was some talk, actually they were pretty much rumors, that he killed some innocent villagers during his tour in Afghanistan while he was in the Army. We heard he'd been given a dishonorable discharge, but when we checked with the Department of Army they said they couldn't locate his file. Stinks if you ask me, but he's got a rock-solid alibi for where he was at the time of Ms. Morton's death. As far as his file being lost, it probably has something to do with the fact everyone knew he was going to be a big football star when he got out of the Army."

"I agree it stinks, but no use pursuing it if he's got an alibi. That's one down. Anything else?"

"I spent a lot of time with contacts of mine in the entertainment industry. Here's what it boils down to. Evidently Jacquie's new picture, The Triangle, was a do or die movie for her as well as pretty much everyone connected with it. After her last movie bombed, this one had to be a hit. The big money men wanted her to play the lead, because they felt she still had drawing power. I understand the director wanted his mistress, Lisette Andrews, to play the lead role, but he was overruled. Everybody associated with the movie was nervous about it, because the rumor is that Jacquie and the screenwriter for the movie weren't getting along. There was talk she wouldn't read any of the revisions to the script he'd written, and she pretty much played the diva around both the screenwriter and Lisette."

"Do you know who chose the screenwriter?"

"Yes, the same money men that wanted Jacquie to play the lead. The director's pretty anxious for a hit as well. Seems like he just missed getting an Oscar and desperately wanted a shot at an Oscar with The Triangle. Looks like a lot of people's futures were riding on the movie, although what's going to happen now, no one could say for sure. There's talk that Lisette Andrews will play the lead, and The Triangle will be made."

"What do you know about her?" Mike asked.

"I've met her at a couple of events, and I like her. I hear she really wanted to play the lead in The Triangle, so she may have had a motive for murdering Jacquie, if, in fact, it turns out she was murdered."

"Hmmm. Did you pick up any rumors about Jacquie's daughter, Kim Morton?"

"Nothing at all that was negative, Mike. Word is that she and her mother tangled over her decision to live in the retreat center run by a guy from India called Guru Dev. I was curious about him, so I had one of my people do a search on him."

"And?" Mike asked.

"From everything my guy could find out, he said Guru Dev is the real deal. He grew up in a small rural village in India, studied yoga and meditation intensely there, and evidently came to the United States at the urging of several people who had studied with him in India and offered to pay his expenses to come here. He ended up in Beverly Hills and started teaching yoga at a high-priced yoga studio one of them owned which catered to people who work in the movie industry.

"That's where Jacquie's daughter met him. He wanted to set up several retreat centers on the West Coast, and when he found out who her mother was he wondered if Kim could introduce him to some people who might be in a position to help him. She said she'd try, but from what we were able to find out, it doesn't look like she's been able to do much in that regard. That's about it, Mike. I don't know if any of this helps, but at least you have a little background info. Let me know if I can do anything else."

"You've done plenty, thanks. Let me know when you're ready for that fishing trip, and I'll arrange it."

"I'll hold you to it. Talk to you soon, and when you do find out whether Jacquie Morton died from natural causes or was murdered, I'd appreciate a phone call."

"You'll be at the top of the list," Mike said as he ended the call.

CHAPTER SEVENTEEN

Early the next morning, Kelly shook her head in disbelief as she got out of her minivan with Rebel and walked over to the front door of the coffee shop. Five people were already standing in front of it, waiting to go in, although officially it wasn't supposed to open until 7:00 a.m., which was still an hour away. She smiled, greeted everyone, and prepared for the day to be just as busy as it had been the day before. Fortunately, the people who were waiting were all regular customers, so she let them in early, and they knew enough to stay out of the staff's way while they started the coffee and got things ready for the day.

Around ten that morning, Kelly realized that Charlie was acting more surly than usual. He was never going to win an award for having an optimistic warm personality, but if possible, today he seemed to be even colder and more withdrawn than he usually was. She walked into the kitchen and said, "Charlie, I've noticed you seem pretty angry this morning. Want to talk about it?"

He looked at her while he made several sandwiches at the same time and said, "I'm okay, but the more time goes by, the angrier I get thinkin' about what happened. Don't seem fair that a beautiful, wonderful woman like Jacquie Morton had to die. She wasn't all that old."

Kelly looked at him closely and realized he was almost on the verge of tears. "I think everyone feels bad about it, Charlie, so you're not alone. Sounds like you might have had some special feelings for her."

"Yeah, me and a lot of other people. You know, we built a movie theater out at the reservation with some of the money we get because of the casino that was built on the reservation. The theater isn't open to the general public, just to members of our tribe, and every Thursday night we show a Jacquie Morton movie. She was my favorite actress, and it wasn't only me, she was a lot of other people's favorite, too."

"How's that casino working out, Charlie? I know your father was very much against having one built on the reservation, but he also told me he was sure when he died the tribe would agree to build it, because so many of the members wanted the money they would get if it was built. Do you think it's helped the members of your tribe?"

"Overall, I'd have to say yes. You know, each member of the tribe gets a monthly allotment from the casino, and believe me, it's a lot of money. Matter of fact, I don't ever have to work again, but I kind of like being the cook here. That money from the casino's allowed us to build our own medical center and school on the reservation, so that's a plus.

"The minus is that because of the large amount of money each member gets every month, some of them don't want to work, and a lot of the kids aren't going to college, even though the tribe will pay for their education. Also, anytime you put together that much money and idle people, drugs and alcohol will soon follow, and we've sure got problems with those. We've hired a couple of counselors who specialize in substance abuse and domestic violence, which also happens a lot on the reservation, so it ain't all roses with that money."

"That's pretty much what your dad was afraid of, and yet he didn't like how poor the members of his tribe were. It's kind of a catch-22 thing, I guess."

"That it is, Kelly, that it is." He paused for a moment, looking out at the diners from his position behind the pass-through window.

"There's that screenwriter that was with Ms. Morton when they had lunch here the other day. Wonder what's going to happen to him now that she won't be starring in the movie?"

Kelly looked out the window and saw Molly seating Mickey Sloan. From the lack of attention the other diners were paying to him, it looked like no one recognized him. She realized famous movie actresses were a lot more visible than screenwriters.

"I better get back out there," she said. "Every table is filled, and Molly and Roxie aren't going to be happy with me if I stay in here much longer. I suppose the only thing I can say about Jacquie Morton is that you're not alone in grieving over her death."

Kelly took a couple of orders from the counter at the pass-through window and delivered them to customers. When she walked by Mickey's table, she stopped and said, "Hello, Mr. Sloan. It's good to see you. I've been wondering what's going to happen to the film you and Jacquie were working on. I know my cook is devastated about her death, because every Thursday they showed one of her films at the theater on the reservation outside of town."

"I got a call last night from the producer, and he told me Lisette Andrews, she's the one who was with Jacquie and me when we ate here a few days ago, is going to have the lead role in it. At least it's still going to be made," he said.

"I imagine that's good news for you. What was Jacquie like? I only met her that one time when the three of you came here for lunch," Kelly said.

He hesitated. "I don't know what was up with Jacquie. I worked on a film with her several years ago, and it was like this Jacquie was a completely different person from the Jacquie I worked with then. This Jacquie found something wrong with everything I wrote, and she never would read her lines in front of me. I still don't understand it, because the next day it was obvious she'd read them, and she'd usually memorized them."

"How do you think you'll like working with Lisette?" Kelly asked.

"I think I'll like it, although she and the director have been an item for quite a few months now." He stopped talking and seemed to be debating whether to tell her something. "Kelly, I understand that your husband is handling the investigation into Jacquie's death. Is that correct?"

"Yes, why?"

"It may be nothing, but yesterday I overheard a phone conversation between Lisette and Teddy James, the director. She had the phone on speaker, because she was putting her hair up in curlers. He was saying something like if anyone asked if he was in the Cedar Bay area the night Jacquie died, to say no. I was in Portland the night Jacquie died, so I didn't know he'd even been here in Cedar Bay.

"My nephew is in the Army, and he's been assigned to a tour of duty in Afghanistan. He was in Portland, had a couple of hours between flights, and I met him at the airport. I hadn't seen him for several years, and I wasn't sure when I was going to see him again, so I made a special trip to Portland to see him. After I met with him I stayed overnight in a hotel there and drove back here to Cedar Bay early the next morning. You can imagine how I felt when I turned on the television news that morning at the hotel while I was getting dressed and learned that Jacquie had died."

"So, you didn't know the director spent the night at your house while you were in Portland visiting your nephew?"

"No, and I don't know why it would be important, but I do think it's strange that Lisette didn't tell me. By the way, Teddy's scheduled to come in this evening to Cedar Bay. The producer is flying up here, too, and we're having a meeting about going forward with the movie and how to change the script to accommodate Lisette. We're also going to discuss who should play the part that previously had been Lisette's."

"Well, it sounds like everything is going forward. I'll tell Mike what you told me, but I have no idea what it has to do with Jacquie's death."

"Nor do I, but for some reason it bothers me."

"Thanks for sharing your concern with me. I see you have a menu and Roxie's making her way over here. By the way, the chili is really good. I fixed it for my husband recently and he loved it, so I feel pretty confident recommending it."

"You've sold me," Mickey said smiling up at her. A moment later Roxie asked if he'd decided what he wanted and he said, "Kelly told me to order the chili, and if that's what the owner recommends, who am I argue with that?"

"Good choice," Roxie said. She wrote it down and walked over to the pass-through window and gave the order to Charlie.

CHAPTER EIGHTEEN

After everyone had finally left, and the coffee shop was closed for the day, Kelly spent an hour prepping things for the following day. She hadn't been able to make any menu items ahead of time like she usually did, because there hadn't been any slow times when she could. She knew if tomorrow was anything like today and yesterday, this was probably the only time she'd be able to do it.

She wondered if Maizie, Jacquie's assistant, had returned to Jacquie's house and how, and if, she'd heard about Jacquie's death. Kelly took Rebel out of the storeroom where he'd been sleeping on the dog bed she kept there for him, and together they drove to Jacquie's house. When she parked in the circular driveway in front of the house, she thought she saw a movement in the living room window, as if someone was looking out of it. She hoped it was Maizie and that she was home.

Kelly left Rebel in the car and walked up the steps to the front porch. She pressed the doorbell and heard it chiming. A few moments later a voice said on the other side of the closed door, "May I help you?"

"Yes. My name is Kelly Reynolds. My husband is Sheriff Mike Reynolds, and he's investigating the death of Jacquie Morton. Are you Maizie?"

The door opened and a small woman with white hair drawn up in a bun on top of her head smoothed her hands on the apron she was wearing and said, "Yes I am. Please come in."

It was the first time Kelly had been in Jacquie Morton's house, and as she looked around, she mentally gave whoever had decorated it high marks for having good taste. She was curious who the decorator was and asked Maizie.

"Ms. Morton flew a decorator up here who she had worked with in Beverly Hills. He knew what she liked and didn't like. He took a lot of photographs and measurements, and a few weeks later he returned with two trucks driven by his employees filled with furniture and decorative objects. They put it all together in a couple of days. When Jacquie arrived, it was completely finished, down to the silverware in the drawer and flowers in every room, just like Ms. Morton liked. He's quite an amazing decorator. Everyone who's anyone in Beverly Hills uses him."

"I can see why. It's very elegant, but at the same time, very warm, and that's a hard combination to achieve."

"May I get you some iced tea, Mrs. Reynolds? I was just going to have some myself."

"Yes, that would be wonderful. Thank you." Kelly followed her into the kitchen, and Maizie gestured for her to have a seat at the kitchen table.

"Now, what do you want from me?" Maizie asked. "My son's a sheriff in Arkansas, so I'm assuming you'd like to know what I know about Ms. Morton."

"Yes, I would. I have a personal interest in this case, because my husband is running for re-election against an opponent who has been accusing my husband of not doing his job properly as the sheriff of Beaver County. He says he would have determined whether Jacquie's death was a homicide or an accident within a matter of hours. He's telling everyone my husband isn't qualified to be the county sheriff, because so far, he hasn't been able to determine if Ms. Morton's death was accidental or the result of some sort of foul play." She paused and took a sip of her iced tea.

"I remember the last time my son ran for re-election," Maizie said. "It was really nasty, so I understand what you're going through. I have to tell you I'm still somewhat in shock about Ms. Morton's death. My daughter and her family live in Portland, and that was one reason I agreed to come up here with Ms. Morton. I wanted to be closer to my family, and being this close to Portland gave me a chance to see them from time to time.

"As a matter of fact, I was there when I learned that she'd died. My granddaughter had to have an emergency appendectomy operation, and Ms. Morton told me to take some time off and go over to Portland, so I could be there with my family. I didn't know anything about her death until after my granddaughter's surgery when I heard about it on the television. I knew there was nothing I could do, so I stayed at my daughter's last night and drove over here this morning."

That means she probably has a pretty good alibi, if it's needed, Kelly thought. "Maizie, can you tell me what Jacquie Morton was like? You probably knew her as well as anyone did. I know she was suffering from macular degeneration. How was that affecting her life?" Kelly asked.

"I'm surprised you know about her eye condition. Ms. Morton was very careful to hide it. She was really afraid of what was happening to her, and she didn't know how she was going to make this movie. She knew it would probably be her last."

"I understand you had become the person Jacquie relied on for most things, since she was unable to see as well as she once could," Kelly said.

"Yes. I was with Ms. Morton when the eye specialist gave her the diagnosis. I remember on the way home telling her we needed to talk about it, and decide how I could best help her. I had been driving her for some time and my job really became one of being her eyes, however and wherever they were needed."

"What kinds of things did you do in addition to driving her?"

"Pretty much anything that involved her having to look at something. I picked out all of her clothes, took her jewelry from the safe, although when I talked to your husband earlier today, he told me there was nothing in the safe when they arrived here at the house after she died. I'm not a law person, but that sure doesn't sound like she died from an accidental fall. I mean where could the jewelry and cash be?

"Anyway, back to your question. Every night I would read her the pages from the script that the screenwriter, Mickey Sloan, had given her earlier in the day, and she would memorize them. Those were probably the major things I did for her."

"It sounds like your job became a lot more difficult and time consuming as her vision began fading."

"Yes, it did," Maizie said. "As a matter of fact, that's pretty much all I did. We had someone come in to clean the house as well as a gardener to take care of the outside. I did the cooking, but other than that, my job was to act as her eyes. I felt sorry for her, because the macular degeneration was not curable. She knew it would only get worse, and that's why she was so intent on making The Triangle movie. She wanted her last movie to be her best, the one people would remember her for."

"I can understand that. I only met her once. You probably know that she hired me to cater a meeting she was going to have the morning after she died. Actually, I was the one who found her. Everybody knows about her being a big star, but what was she really like?"

Maizie took a long sip of her iced tea and looked out the window. She turned back to Kelly and said, "She was a difficult woman. I worked for her for many, many years, and I saw her change from a very happy young woman who wanted nothing more than to be a star, to becoming a star and demanding star treatment from everyone. Really, I think there were only two people who didn't treat her like a star."

"Who would they be?"

"Her daughter, Kim, and me. For some reason, she felt very comfortable with me, probably because of our long relationship. Kim never cared about being a movie star's daughter, and she hated it when people fawned all over her just so they could have access to her mother. Kim and her mother were at the opposite extremes of what makes people happy. Rather than money and fame, Kim chose the life of a spiritual seeker. As a matter of fact, she doesn't live too far away. She's at Guru Dev's Loving Care Retreat Center. Unfortunately, her mother could not understand why she was so interested in things like yoga and meditation. They became somewhat estranged because of Kim's involvement in Guru Dev's center."

"From what you're telling me, it seems they definitely were miles apart. How would you define their relationship at the time of Jacquie's death?"

Maizie twisted her hands in her lap and said very quietly, "It was not good. They had a major argument several days before Ms. Morton died, and when Kim left the house that day she was very angry." Maizie looked like she wanted to say more, but she stopped talking.

"Can you tell me what they were arguing about? I know it's none of my business, but anything you can tell me might help my husband solve the mystery surrounding Jacquie's death. If your son, the sheriff, is married, I'm sure his wife would do everything she could to help him, so that's why I'm trying to help my husband."

"Yes, he is married, and yes, she would want to help him." Maize sighed and took another sip of her iced tea. Her long fingers were wrapped around the glass, and her knuckles were white from gripping it so tightly. That was the only sign Kelly could see that indicated the stress Maizie was obviously under.

She began to speak. "Kim wanted Ms. Morton to give her an early inheritance. You see, Kim was Ms. Morton's only child, and she was the heir to Ms. Morton's sizable fortune. Kim saw no reason why Ms. Morton couldn't give her a large amount of money now, so she could give it to Guru Dev, and it would allow him to open more yoga and meditation centers. Ms. Morton told Kim that he was a quack, and the only reason he wanted her to live in his seedy commune, those were the words Ms. Morton used, was so he could get Kim to ask her for money.

"Kim was furious and said something like how would Ms. Morton know what his retreat center was like since she'd never bothered to even go out to it, although Kim had asked her to visit several times. That's pretty much the nuts and bolts of it. They did not part on good terms, and unless she and Kim spoke while I was gone, those might have been the last words they ever said to each other."

"That's really sad. As a parent, I hate to hear about parents and children who have become estranged. It seems unnatural to me," Kelly said. "Did they talk about anything else before the argument?"

"I don't know. When Kim came, she admired the flowers that our gardener, Jose Hernandez, had planted a few days earlier. I told her and Ms. Morton about how his wife had just been diagnosed with ALS and that it was incurable. I told them how worried he was. They were both sorry because he's been the gardener here ever since Ms. Morton bought this house. He'd asked me to give the flowers a little extra water, so I left the two of them to go outside. When I heard raised voices, I walked into the house to see what was wrong. That's when I overheard the conversation I just told you about."

"What do you know about the gardener?" Kelly asked, thinking of what Roger Babowal had told her regarding the gardener looking in the window for longer that he thought was appropriate.

"I've always found Juan to be a very nice young man. One time he and I were talking about food, and he told me his wife, Serena, made the best tamales he'd ever tasted. He asked me if I would like to go to their home and join them for lunch some Sunday after church. We all attended the same church, well, Ms. Morton didn't go to church, but I did. Anyway, I went to their home for lunch and he was right. The tamales were fabulous. I'd met his wife and three daughters at church, but I hadn't talked very much to them before I went to their home. There was so much love and happiness in that home, even if they didn't have many material things by a lot of people's standards.

"I really feel sorry for all of them what with Serena being diagnosed with ALS," Maizie said as she stood up. "I hope what I've told you helps. I spoke with Ms. Morton's attorney a little while ago, and he asked me to make a list of the things in the house I thought were valuable. He said he's trying to get an idea of the value of Ms. Morton's estate, so he can begin to probate it."

"I really appreciate you taking the time to talk to me and answer my questions. If you don't mind, I have one more. Do you know if Kim is the sole beneficiary of Jacquie's estate? You mentioned you thought she was her only heir."

"I don't know for sure. The attorney didn't say anything to me about that. Ms. Morton may have changed her trust, but I don't think so, although she threatened Kim that she might cut her out of her estate if she didn't leave that seedy commune. Ms. Morton's attorney's office is in Los Angeles, and unless he flew up here when I was in Portland, and she created a new trust, which I think is very doubtful, yes, I think Kim would still be the sole beneficiary."

"Again, thank you so much, Maizie. Here's my phone number. If you think of anything you feel might be important, please call me. I'll leave you to your list making. What are you going to do now?" Kelly asked as they walked to the front door.

"My daughter wants me to move to Portland and live near her family. Ms. Morton paid me very well over the years, and I've saved most of it, so I really don't have to work. I think I'll probably buy a condominium or a small house and settle near them."

"I wish you well," Kelly said as she smiled at Maizie and walked out the front door.

CHAPTER NINETEEN

Kelly had almost reached her minivan when she heard a voice say, "Kelly, do you have a minute?"

She looked over and saw Roger Babowal waving to her from his backyard and motioning to her. "Be right there," she said as she walked over to where he was standing with his dog, Rusty, at his side.

"Sorry to bother you. I'm glad I saw you, because I've been wondering if I should call you. You saved me the trouble."

"Did you remember something more about Jacquie Morton or the night she died?" Kelly asked.

"It may be absolutely nothing, but I thought it was odd. The night she died I remember seeing a black Mercedes pulling into the driveway of the house on the other side of Jacquie Morton's house. I know a screenwriter who was working on the script for her new movie and a woman who was going to be in the movie, are living in that house, so a Mercedes in the driveway wouldn't be all that strange. But here's what I think is interesting. I take Rusty out for a walk very early in the morning, like around 4:30 or so. It's a curse of old age thing. I just can't sleep in like I used to. Sorry, I'm digressing. Anyway, when we went out that morning, the car was gone. It was still there when I took Rusty out for his last visit to the yard the evening before, so I thought it was odd that someone would leave either really late or really early."

"I agree. I know this is a long shot, but when the car pulled into the driveway, did you happen to see who got out of it?" Kelly asked.

"I did, and I thought he looked familiar, but I couldn't place him. You know, one of those things that drives you nuts when you can't remember it, and then you wake up at 3:00 a.m. and bingo, there's the answer. Well, here's the answer. Chris, my wife, was out of town when the Oscars were on television a couple of months ago, and she made me promise I'd tape the show for her, which I did. We both kind of forgot about it, and recently I remembered and reminded her that I'd taped it for her. She watched the show several nights ago. I was reading a book, and I glanced at the show from time to time, although they don't interest me much. Isn't really my thing, but I'm pretty sure the guy I saw getting out of the car at the screenwriter's house was a director who'd been nominated for an Oscar but didn't win."

"Thank you so much, Roger. I have no idea if it's relevant, but I agree with you, it does sound odd. I'll tell my husband, and maybe he can make something of it. You have my number. Please call me if you think of anything else. It may not seem like much to you, but it might be just the thing my husband needs to help him solve the mystery surrounding Jacquie Morton's death."

Kelly reached down and petted Rusty, regretting she'd left Rebel in her minivan. She knew how much he enjoyed interacting with other dogs. A moment later she stood up to leave and had taken a few steps toward her minivan when Roger said in a hesitating voice, "Kelly, there may be something else. I noticed a car driving along the road when I was outside that night, and since we don't get too many cars here at that time of night, it caught my attention. I looked at it fairly closely when it slowly passed by me. The dome light inside the car was on, you know, kind of like when you're looking at a map or an address. I'd swear I saw a guy wearing a turban sitting in the passenger seat. I mean, it's pretty strange to see anyone wearing a turban in this sleepy little town, so that definitely caught my attention. In fact, I think it was a first for me. Cedar Bay is not a tourist attraction for people from other countries. Don't know if that'll help your husband, but thought I ought to tell you."

Roger looked down at his dog and said, "Rusty, time to go in. We've taken up enough of Kelly's time." He gave her a slight wave, and the two of them walked in the back door of his house.

Kelly stood there for a moment, unsure what to make of the latest bit of information Roger Babowal had just given her. *A man wearing a turban in front of Jacquie's home the night she died. The only man I can think of who would be wearing a turban and driving by Jacquie Morton's house is Guru Dev. Could he have possibly talked to Jacquie or…*

She didn't like the answer her mind was coming up with and decided it was time to pay a visit the seedy commune, as Jacquie Morton had called it.

CHAPTER TWENTY

Guru Dev's spiritual retreat center, known as The Loving Care Retreat Center, was located about ten miles east of Cedar Bay, and Kelly easily drove to it. She remembered when she and Mike had driven by it several months earlier that there was a large sign with the name of the center on it next to a guard gate. She stopped her minivan at the gate and rolled down her window. A man in a white tunic and pants stepped out of the small building and said, "This is private property. May I help you?"

"Yes, I'd like to see Kim Morton. My name is Kelly Reynolds. You might tell her it's regarding her mother."

"I'll be back in a minute. I need to call her and get permission for you to enter the property, but the dog will have to stay in your car."

"I understand. Thank you."

She watched as the young man talked to someone on his cell phone. After a few minutes, he walked out of the small building and said, "Kim said you can come in. She'll be waiting for you at the top of the hill. Just follow this road. The main part of the center is up about a mile. You can't miss it."

"Thanks," Kelly said as she started up the road. A few minutes later she rounded a curve and saw a number of small cottages beyond what appeared to be the main building for the center that the young man had referred to. A young woman was standing next to it and waved to her. She motioned for Kelly to follow her as she began walking to a small cabin at the far end of the area. Kelly parked in front of it, told Rebel to stay, and got out of her minivan.

"Hi, you must be Kim. My name is Kelly Reynolds. Thanks for agreeing to see me."

"Nice meeting you, Mrs. Reynolds. Let's go into my cabin. We can talk a little more privately in there."

She opened the door and motioned for Kelly to go ahead of her. Kelly walked in and had a hard time believing what she was seeing. She'd read about some children of wealthy parents who had chosen to renounce the material world in which their parents lived, but this was the first time she'd actually experienced it. The room was devoid of anything personal. It had a cot which was about as severe looking as any bed Kelly had ever seen, a meditation pillow, candles, and incense. There were five pegs on the wall where a coat, three white tunics, and a bathrobe hung. There was a one-drawer cabinet in the corner where Kelly assumed Kim kept the few personal items she needed, such as the loose white cotton pants she wore with the matching tunic that completed her outfit. Other than that, the small one-room cabin was bare.

"You can see that I've chosen not to be a part of the world that my mother lived in," Kim said. "I met Guru Dev, he's the head of The Loving Care Retreat Center, at a yoga class several years ago. I became his disciple, and when he opened this center, I came here to live and study with him. He's absolutely the most wonderful human being I've ever met. I'd heard of mystics who had special powers, but I wasn't sure I believed it. After meeting Guru Dev and studying with him, I definitely believe some people have certain types of extraordinary powers, and he's one of them. He knows exactly what I'm thinking without me ever saying anything," she said smiling.

"I've heard the same thing," Kelly said, "but like you, I've not met anyone who has those powers. From the looks of this center, it seems that there are a number of people who have come here to study with him."

"Yes. Presently he has sixty-three disciples living here. He's developed quite a reputation, and every day he turns down people, because there's no room for any more people to live here at the center. As a matter of fact, he was recently written up in one of the top yoga and meditation magazines as being the number one leader in his field. You can imagine how many people have tried to come here just from that magazine article alone."

"You must be one of the lucky ones, because you seem to have discovered him before the rest of that community did," Kelly said.

"I consider myself to be the luckiest person in the world. To study yoga and meditation with him is all I ever want to do. He has made me the second in command here at the center. There are so many people who want to study with him that Guru Dev and I are constantly discussing ways we can expand this center and even build more, but money is always a problem," Kim said.

Privately Kelly wondered if the reason Guru Dev had made Kim second in command was because of who her mother was. It was well-known that Jacquie Morton had been one of the wealthiest actresses in the movie industry. Kelly liked the young woman and sincerely hoped for her sake that Guru Dev was honorable and not a fraud. She knew Mike was going to talk to the Beverly Hills police chief today, and she assumed he'd ask the chief what he knew about the spiritual leader.

Kim motioned for Kelly to sit on the cot while she gracefully lowered herself onto her meditation pillow in one fluid movement. Kelly wished she could do something like that, but she knew at her age it took a bit more flexibility than she had to get up and down like that from the floor, and it certainly didn't happen in one graceful movement like Kim was able to do.

"My husband is Sheriff Mike Reynolds. I believe he's the one who told you about the death of your mother. I'd like to express my condolences. Losing a mother is not an easy thing. The reason I'm here is that my husband is in a very contested election in his race for re-election as the sheriff of Beaver County. I'm trying to take a little of the pressure off of him and see if I can find out anything from the people who knew your mother that might help him determine the circumstances surrounding her death. I'm not in law enforcement, I'm just a woman trying to help her husband. If you can think of anything that might be relevant to your mother's death, I'd really appreciate it."

"I don't know anything about how she died," Kim said. "I'd visited her a few days before she was found dead. The next thing I knew was when I got the phone call from your husband about her death. Because of my involvement with Guru Dev, my mother and I were not particularly close the last few years."

"I understand there's going to be a large funeral in Los Angeles for her," Kelly said. "I believe I read in the paper that her agent feels it's imperative to hold one in order to give her fans a chance to publicly mourn her death. Will you be attending it?"

"I have absolutely no desire to go and be subjected to the world I've chosen to distance myself from, but Guru Dev is insistent that I attend her funeral. He doesn't want to draw attention to the retreat center, and he's afraid if I don't go to the funeral, the retreat center could become the target of bad publicity. He thinks the media might write that The Loving Care Retreat Center is some sort of a cult, that I was being held against my will here, and that the cult prevented me from attending my mother's funeral."

"I think that's probably wise advice. Do you have any brothers or sisters?"

"No, I'm an only child. Actually, my mother had me out of wedlock, and to this day I don't know the identity of my real father. When my mother was married to Deke Cannon, he wanted to adopt me, but my mother refused. Since they ended up getting divorced, she probably made the right decision. If I'd been his stepdaughter, it would have made it all that much messier. He was always very good to me, and I still talk to him once in a while, although I never let my mother know that."

"Kim, I hate to sound crass, and I know this is none of my business, but since you appear to have taken a vow of poverty, and I assume you will be the one to inherit the majority, if not all of your mother's estate, what do you intend to do with the money?"

"That's kind of a no-brainer, Mrs. Reynolds. I'll give it all to Guru Dev, of course, so he can build more retreat centers."

"Kim, again, this is none of my business, but I can't help asking how you think your mother would feel about that?"

"Quite frankly, Mrs. Reynolds, Guru Dev is alive, and my mother is dead. When I inherit the money, it will be mine to do with it as I wish. I can see from the look on your face that you're not sure that's the right thing for me to do. I'd like to introduce you to Guru Dev, and then you'll understand why I decided to become his disciple. He's usually free at this time of day. Come with me, please, and you can meet him in person," she said as she stood up in one graceful movement.

CHAPTER TWENTY-ONE

A few minutes later, Kim knocked on the door of a cabin much like the one she lived in and entered when a soft voice said, "Please come in." Kelly and Kim walked into the cabin, and it was evident to Kelly that Guru Dev was not setting himself apart from his disciples by living in some mansion while they lived spartan lives in their cabins.

"Guru Dev, this is Mrs. Reynolds. Her husband is the sheriff of Beaver County and he was the one who informed me of my mother's death. She's trying to help him by seeing if she can find anything out regarding the circumstances of my mother's death."

Kelly had taken yoga classes on and off at the White Cloud Retreat Center and knew that the proper greeting when meeting someone like Guru Dev was to put one's hands together in a prayer position above the heart, bow one's head, and say "Namaste," which she did. Guru Dev returned the greeting and motioned for them to sit on cushions on the floor. It took Kelly a little longer than it did Kim, but finally they were seated.

"I understand you are interested in opening more retreat centers like this one, Guru Dev," Kelly said. "Can you tell me a little more about your plans?"

His words came slowly, and it was obvious English was not his native language. He told her about his plans for more retreat centers and how many more people wanted to study with him. Guru Dev spoke factually, and Kelly didn't detect any signs that he was the least bit egotistical. She could only assume that what he was saying was true. He needed more places to teach the people who wanted to study with him. It was as simple as that.

He introduced Kelly to a young man named Jonah, who had been in the room with him when they'd arrived. Guru Dev asked Jonah to bring tea to them. A few moments later he returned with a tray carrying a teapot and cups.

As he passed the tea, Guru Dev said, "We practice veganism here at the center, so no milk products are used. My studies have proven to me that sugar is not a good thing to put into one's body, so that too is prohibited. We drink our herbal tea without either."

"Actually, this is exactly how I like my tea," Kelly said. "It's delicious."

While they sipped their tea, Guru Dev said, "Mrs. Reynolds, I have told Kim how very sorry I am about her mother. I never met her, although I tried to once. I actually had Jonah drive me to her home. As it turned out, we drove by her house the very night she died."

"I didn't know that. Why did you go there, Guru Dev?" Kim asked, seeming genuinely surprised by his revelation.

"I didn't want to put you in the middle of something, Kim. I thought maybe if I spoke directly to your mother, she would loan me money for the retreat centers I want to build. Actually, it was late at night when I made my decision, and I asked Jonah to drive me to her home. When Jonah and I were in front of your mother's home trying to make sure we had the right house, a fancy looking black car backed out of the driveway of the house next to hers and almost hit our car. The person driving the car drove away really fast and what I would consider to be in a reckless manner. I decided it was a bad omen, and I told Jonah to take me back to the center."

"Do you know what kind of a car it was?" Kelly asked.

The spiritual leader shook his head indicating that he didn't. Jonah spoke up. "It was a new Mercedes Benz. I'm familiar with that model, because my father has one like it."

Kim turned to Kelly and said, "Jonah and I have pretty much grown up together. We lived across the street from each other in Beverly Hills, and we've always been very close. His parents and my mother were good friends. His father is an investment adviser who deals mainly with movie stars, so we knew a lot of the same people. When I began to take yoga from Guru Dev, I told Jonah how wonderful Guru Dev was, and I urged Jonah to start studying with him as well. He did, and then we both moved up here to live with him at the retreat center."

When she'd finished speaking, Guru Dev said, "Mrs. Reynolds, thank you for coming. I hope you found out something that will help your husband. Please excuse me, but it is getting close to the time for me to do my meditation practice. Kim, would you stay here for a moment? I would like to talk to you about a few things we need to do here at the center. Jonah, please escort Mrs. Reynolds to her car."

The traditional Namaste greeting again took place, and Kelly and Jonah walked out the door and over to her minivan where Rebel was watching every movement she made. "Jonah, I'd like to ask you something, and if you choose not to answer me, I'll understand, but I'm curious. Are you in love with Kim? Is that why you decided to come here?"

"Is it that obvious?" he asked with an abashed look on his face.

"I'm an experienced observer of human nature, and the way you were looking at Kim indicated to me that although she may think of you as a friend, you'd prefer that the relationship was a little different."

"You're very astute, Mrs. Reynolds. I thought I hid it better than that. Yes, I followed her here for two reasons. One, I'm in love with her and secondly, I've been concerned about her obsession with Guru Dev, although based on what he told me this morning, there was no reason for me to be concerned."

"What did he tell you that caused you to change your mind?"

"Kim has told me several times that he has powers other people don't have. She always said he could read her mind. Well, he read mine this morning. He told me he was aware Kim was infatuated with him, but that I needn't worry. Guru Dev said he had taken a vow of celibacy, and he had no romantic interest in any of his devotees or anyone else. Then he looked at me and said, 'Jonah, you and Kim are meant for each other, and you will soon be together in the way you want to be. The time is coming near.' I don't know exactly what that means, Mrs. Reynolds, but I was happy to hear it."

"Thank you for telling me, Jonah, and I wish you and Kim the best of luck."

CHAPTER TWENTY-TWO

When Kelly and Rebel got home, she saw Mike's car in the driveway. She remembered he'd told her he was giving a speech to the Chamber of Commerce that evening, and she mentally went through a list of what was available in the refrigerator that she could use to make a quick dinner for him before he had to leave. She was anxious to tell him about her day and curious if he'd found out anything.

She opened the door and was greeted by Lady and Skyy, tails wagging in anticipation of dinner. "Kelly, I'm in the bedroom changing clothes. I'll be with you in a minute," she heard Mike say in a loud voice.

"Take your time. I need to pull a couple of things out of the refrigerator, so I can make dinner and get you to your meeting on time," she answered.

She fed the dogs and surveyed the refrigerator, deciding that Mike's meeting called for a soup and sandwich dinner. She'd made a cream of mushroom soup a couple of days earlier and decided it would go well with some turkey burgers she had in the freezer that were to be cooked while they were still frozen. That problem taken care of, she filled two glasses with iced tea, picked several sprigs of mint from some herbs she kept in pots on the kitchen windowsill, and added them to the iced tea. She'd just finished when Mike walked into the kitchen, kissed her lightly on the cheek, and took the glass of iced tea she handed him.

"Well, my love, how was everything at the coffee shop today? One of my deputies tried to eat lunch there and had to leave, since he couldn't find anywhere to sit. He said it was standing room only, and he didn't have time to stand and wait for a seat. He was in a time crunch, because I sent out a memo this morning telling everyone I was holding a mandatory meeting in the conference room to discuss the status of the Jacquie Morton case at 1:00 this afternoon.

"He said to tell you that you have absolutely no competition from the fast food restaurant that recently opened down the street from Kelly's. He made a point of telling everyone in the room that your cook, Charlie, made the best chili burger in the county and maybe even the state. Thought you'd like to hear what he had to say. Money can't buy word of mouth advertising like that."

"The coffee shop was crazy today, Mike, and what's interesting is that many of the customers were from out of town. I'm sure they were here in Cedar Bay because of Jacquie's death. The screenwriter who was working on her script came in today for lunch, and I had a conversation with him."

Mike raised an eyebrow. "I'm certainly hoping it was strictly a customer speaking to a coffee shop owner type of conversation, not one involving Jacquie's death or anything about her, but knowing you, you probably better tell me about it."

Kelly stirred the soup and then sat down at the kitchen table across from him. "Well, the conversation did veer a little in the direction of Jacquie's death, but given that he was working with her, that's not surprising," she said innocently with a wide-eyed look on her face. "Here's what he had to say about her."

"I would prefer it if you had stuck to telling him about Charlie's chili burgers, but from what you've told me time and time again, these conversations just seem to happen when you're around, and they're usually with someone who has information about a case I'm working on. Would I be right?"

"That you would be, Sheriff, and while I'm at it, you'd probably like to hear about my conversations with Jacquie's daughter and her administrative assistant.

"For the record, before you even start, I'm going to register a complaint. It's one thing to have the screenwriter come in for lunch, but from what I've heard about the retreat center, the people who live there don't come into town except for supplies, and I rather doubt that the coffee shop is on their list of places to visit if they do come into town. I also don't think Jacquie's assistant would be inclined to stop by the coffee shop when she goes into town, which means none of them came to you. You went out to Jacquie's house and The Loving Care Retreat Center, right, although you did mention that you were going to, and I believe I asked for your opinion."

"Well, hmmm, yes. I don't think I actually planned on talking to them about Jacquie, but you see, I got so concerned about your re-election and all that you're trying to do, I thought maybe I could help you by seeing what I could find out."

"Somehow, I'm missing the logic in that segue, but then again, my love, I can't say that logic has ever been your strong suit. So, tell me what you found out," he said, taking a drink from his glass of iced tea.

She told him about her visit with Maizie and then about driving out to The Loving Care Retreat Center. She also told him about her conversation with Roger Babowal. When she finished, she said, "Mike, Maizie certainly confirmed what Doc and Liz told us about Jacquie's failing eyesight.

"I thought it was interesting that Mr. Babowal saw a man wearing a turban in a car that happened to be outside Jacquie's house on the night she died. I didn't get a sense that Guru Dev had anything to do with Jacquie's death, and Jonah pretty much confirmed that they drove back to the center and never stopped at her home. As far as the black Mercedes car that Roger, Guru Dev, and Jonah saw, I have no idea who it belonged to."

"Your instincts were probably right on concerning Guru Dev," Mike said. "I had a long talk this afternoon with my friend who's the Beverly Hills police chief, and he told me that from the research his staff did on him, he seems to be the real deal. They didn't find anything that would indicate he was a scam artist."

"I'm glad, but I wonder about Kim. You haven't told me yet whether the coroner has made a determination as to whether Jacquie's death was accidental or the result of foul play, but let's say she was murdered. You always say to look at who has the most to gain when it comes to a reason why someone would commit murder. Mike, I see your raised hand, and I know you're going to tell me that there's no evidence she was murdered, but if she was, her daughter seems to have the most to gain. Maybe she killed her mother to get her inheritance so she could give it to Guru Dev, hoping to show what a good disciple she is and curry favor with him. She did tell me she planned on giving her inheritance to him."

"Kelly, I did talk to the coroner, who as you well know, is certainly not one of my favorite people. He told me he's been too busy to get around to doing the necessary tests on Jacquie. Be my bet he's too busy stuffing his mouth with donuts or some other food. I wouldn't even put it past him to delay the autopsy on Jacquie hoping I'll get some bad publicity from it and lose the election," he said dejectedly. "Who knows, maybe he's working with my opponent."

"Could be, but the good news is that if he doesn't like you at least he doesn't come to Kelly's Koffee Shop. That's a blessing, because I'd have a hard time being civil to him or serving him."

"Thanks for your support, my love. The chief also cleared Jacquie's ex-husband, Deke Cannon. One of the chief's staff talked to the manager of the restaurant where he works, and he was working there on the night of Jacquie's death. There's no way he could have been in Cedar Bay and Beverly Hills at the same time."

"So, let's think about this, and I know this is still very much conjecture, and she could have simply misjudged the distance to the edge of the cliff, but so far it sounds to me like you've eliminated

Guru Dev and Jacquie's ex-husband. That still leaves Mickey, the screenwriter, Lisette, who will now have the lead role, the gardener, and even her daughter. Can you think of anyone else?"

"No, Kelly, I, and I emphasize the word I, cannot think of anyone else, and I don't want you to think about it at all. For one thing, what if Jacquie was murdered? The way you're talking to people, if you should discover something, knowingly or unknowingly, you could become the murderer's next victim. Seriously, Kelly, I'm not asking you, I'm begging you. Please don't try to help me anymore. I appreciate what you've done, but that's enough. The thing is I love you more than anything, and if keeping you away from potential murderers causes me to lose the election, oh well. I've got a nice pension, and I might just make a great waiter at your coffee shop. We'll be fine. No more helping me, promise?"

"I promise, Mike," she said, glad that she'd decided long ago to skip the weekly confession with Father Brown at the Catholic Church in Cedar Bay. She was certain Mike wouldn't approve of the plan she'd come up with, but she justified it by reasoning that although Mike hadn't often been happy about the choices she'd made to help him solve his cases in the past, they'd always helped.

"Kelly, think I better eat and get ready for my speech at the Chamber of Commerce meeting tonight. Any chance you can come with me?"

"I'd really like to, Mike," she said deliberately avoiding his gaze by keeping busy searing the turkey burgers and stirring the soup, "but as busy as it was today at the coffee shop, I never had a chance to do the prep work that I usually do on and off during the day for the following day or, in this case, Monday. I thought I'd go into Kelly's for a couple of hours this evening and try to get caught up. I have no reason to think Monday won't be just as busy as today was."

"I understand," he said picking up his spoon as she set the soup and sandwich on the table in front of him. "I would ask one thing of you, though. I'm well aware that the cause of Jacquie's death is still up in the air, but humor me by taking Rebel with you when you go back to the coffee shop this evening, okay?"

"Sure, happy to. He's always good company."

"One last thing, Kelly, keep the doors on your minivan locked and lock the coffee shop door after you and Rebel are inside."

"For you, my love, anything. Consider it done, and good luck tonight, although I know you won't need it."

CHAPTER TWENTY-THREE

Kelly didn't want to lie to Mike any more than she felt was absolutely necessary to help him solve the mystery surrounding Jacquie's death, so she and Rebel went to Kelly's Koffee Shop, just like she'd told him she was planning on doing. She spent an hour getting ready for the crowd she expected on Monday. As always, she mentally thanked the restaurant gods for sending Charlie, Roxie, and Molly to her. She knew without them, she never would have survived the week.

"Okay, Rebel, time to go. I want to pay a visit to Mickey Sloan. I think there's more for me to learn there." She locked the door of the coffee shop, and after she and Rebel got in her minivan, she locked those doors as well.

She didn't want to draw attention to herself or the minivan when she paid a visit to Mickey Sloan, so she parked in a nearby cutout overlooking the ocean. It was a short walk to the house where Mickey was living. When they walked past Roger Babowal's home she saw the tip of a lit cigarette in the darkness next to his house. A moment later she heard his voice ask, "Kelly, what are you doing here at this time of night? If I were your husband I wouldn't want you to be by yourself at night in an area where a woman recently died under possibly suspicious circumstances."

She and Rebel walked over to where Rusty and Roger were standing. "I take it your wife is watching television or something."

"That she is, and it provided a perfect opportunity for me to take Rusty outside, and I'd be remiss if I didn't say it also provides an opportunity for me to have a cigarette. I've tried and tried to give them up, but once in a while I feel I can justify one. Anyway, why are you here?"

"I just have a feeling that I'm overlooking something. I don't know, maybe it's my woman's intuition. Anyway, I had a strong sense I needed to come back here and see if I've missed something. Roger, as far as my husband being worried, Mike always worries about me. If there's even a hint that I might be in danger, he insists I take Rebel with me everywhere I go."

"Sounds like a good idea to me. Mind if I accompany you?"

"No, I could probably use another pair of eyes."

"Give me one minute. I want to put Rusty in the house. He's not used to things like this. I'll be right back."

When he returned, she said, "Roger, I have no idea what I'm even looking for. I want to talk to Mickey, the screenwriter. He came in the coffee shop today, and for some reason, I feel he has additional information he didn't share with me. Let's not talk anymore until we see what's happening. I don't want our voices to be heard." She saw him nod as they walked silently to Mickey's nearby house.

Kelly noticed there was a large black car in Mickey's driveway. She didn't know much about cars, but she thought it was a Mercedes Benz. She remembered what Roger had said about a man he'd thought was a director getting out of a car that was similar to this one on the night of Jacquie Morton's death. Jonah had also said the car that almost hit his when it rapidly backed out of Mickey's driveway was a Mercedes. Kelly thought that was a lot of coincidences and when it came to people dying, she shared Mike's dislike of coincidences. Mike was a strong believer that there were no coincidences when death was involved.

The homeowners of the upscale residential area had asked the city not to install streetlights, so they could maintain the illusion that they were living in a rural area. It was very dark as they approached Mickey's house. With Rebel by her side, Kelly took Roger's hand, and they quietly walked towards a window which was illuminated by a light from within.

As they looked in the window which was slightly ajar, Kelly recognized Lisette, the woman who was now going to be starring as the lead in The Triangle. She was talking to a man whose back was to the window. Kelly didn't recognize him, but she heard Roger gasp. "That's Teddy James, that director I saw on the Oscar show," he whispered.

The man halfway turned, and Kelly saw that he was holding a diamond necklace and a pair of large diamond earrings in his hand. The man began to speak and they both heard him say, "Lisette, these are for you. Now that Jacquie's gone, you're going to be the most famous actress in the world. I got these for you to show you how much faith I have in you and how much I love you. Turn around and let me put the necklace on you, then you can put the earrings on. I don't think I'd be any good at putting them on you."

Lisette turned her back to him, so he could hook the necklace around her neck. She picked up a mirror to look at the necklace once the man had secured it on her neck. From where Kelly was standing she could see Lisette's reflection in the mirror. Lisette's eyes widened, and her expression changed. "Teddy, where did you get these? I know I've seen them before."

"It doesn't matter where I got them, sweetheart. They're yours now. You were made for jewels, and when I saw them they made me think of you. By giving these to you, I pledge to make you a star. What's important is you, and these are just the first of many gifts I intend to shower you with."

Lisette stepped back from him, whirled around, and said, "You killed Jacquie, didn't you? This jewelry is hers, isn't it? You were here the night she died. I remember you said you had to make an important phone call and then you went outside. You told me you didn't want to bore me by having me listen to your end of the conversation. When you came back in you told me you had to leave immediately. I'm right about you murdering her, aren't I."

"So, what if you are? The thing is you're here, and Jacquie's gone. You're going to be a big star, Lisette, even bigger than Jacquie was. I promise. Don't make this into a big deal. Anyway, this would have been Jacquie's last movie even if she had lived. She had macular degeneration, and she was losing her eyesight. That's why she never would read the scripts in front of Mickey and you. She couldn't make out the words on the script. Lisette, I killed Jacquie Morton for you and your career, and yes, ultimately for the two of us. Don't worry, there were no witnesses., and no one will ever know I did it.

"It was easy enough to do. I just went next door and rang her doorbell. She let me in because she recognized my voice. I held a gun on her while I cleaned out the cash and jewelry she had in her wall safe. Then I forced her to walk out the back door of the house. She couldn't see how close she was to the edge of the cliff. I gave her a hard shove in the back, and over she went. It was finished and done in less than a couple of minutes. Jacquie never would have been able to make The Triangle worthy of an Academy Award, but you can. What are you doing?" he shouted as Lisette ran past him towards the door.

Teddy hurried after her and grabbed her arm. "Lisette, don't do this. This is your big chance. Without this movie and me, you'll end up being an actress in B movies, if that. In a few years, you'll be stuck working as a waitress, hoping against hope that your agent, if you still have one, can get you a nothing role in a nothing movie."

Lisette and Teddy had made their way out of the house and were only a few feet away from where Kelly, Roger, and Rebel were standing in the shadows. Kelly felt a movement from Roger and heard him say in a loud voice, "Let her go. I've got a gun on you. Put your hands up, then lie down on the ground, arms in front of you." Kelly looked over in amazement at the gun in Roger Babowal's hand.

"Rebel, on guard," she said as Rebel raced over to where Teddy was kneeling, preparing to lie down on the ground. "Rebel, stay." The big dog knew from his training when he'd been the drug enforcement officer's dog what that meant. He put his big, strong paws on Teddy's back, pinning him to the ground and snarling in a menacing manner.

Kelly took her phone out of her pocket and called Mike. "Good timing, Kelly," he said. "I just finished my speech, and I think it went well. What's up?"

"I have some good news for you. I don't know if you have a stage or a microphone at your meeting, but you might want to use both if you do and tell the Chamber of Commerce members that Jacquie Morton was murdered, and the man who did it has been caught. We're at the house next door to Jacquie's, you know, the one the screenwriter is living in. The man who murdered her is the famous director, Teddy James. Tell everyone that Sheriff Mike Reynolds is responsible for the killer being caught. We'll wait for you, but try to hurry."

"Who's the we?" he asked in a grim voice.

"Me, Jacquie's next door neighbor, Roger Babowal, and Rebel. Roger has a gun on him, and Rebel's on guard.

"Well, I don't know how much experience Mr. Babowal has with a gun, but I sure know how much experience Rebel has with helping take care of killers. Think you're in good hands. I'll call Brandon, my deputy. He can get there a lot faster than I can. Just stay put."

Five minutes later the sound of sirens filled the air. Brandon threw his car door open, ran over to Kelly, and said, "You okay, Mrs. Reynolds?" Several deputies surrounded Teddy James, who was quickly handcuffed and placed in a nearby patrol car.

"Yes, Brandon, I'm fine."

About the same time the back door to Mickey's house flew open, and he came running out. "I was in the back of the house doing some laundry when I heard sirens. Lisette, what's going on?" he asked. He noticed she was shaking, and he put his arm around her. "What happened?"

"Teddy killed Jacquie. He admitted it to me. Mrs. Reynolds and this man also heard him admit it. Oh, Mickey, I can't believe I was in love with a murderer. This is horrible."

"Ma'am, I'm sorry, but I'm going to have to take a statement from all of you, including you sir," Brandon said, gesturing towards Mickey. "Why don't we go inside, where we can be a little more comfortable."

Fifteen minutes later Mike arrived. He'd been on the phone with his deputies and knew that Lisette, Mickey, Roger, and Kelly were in the house while Brandon was taking statements from them. "Kelly, I'm not going to have everyone listen to this again, but when we get home I'd be curious as to how you just happened to end up at this particular house when you told me you were going to the coffee shop. I'd also be curious how you happened to hear Teddy James admit he killed Jacquie. And you, sir," he said as he turned towards Roger, "I am very curious how you just happened to be with my wife and how you happened to have a gun with you. I'm sure you can understand why I feel a little out of the loop here."

"Sheriff, I got statements from Kelly and Ms. Andrews, and I was just about to ask those same questions of Mr. Babowal," Brandon said.

Everyone turned expectantly towards Roger Babowal who began to talk. "Well, Rusty, my dog, and I were outside and happened to see Kelly and Rebel walking down the street. I called her over and asked her what she was doing. She explained she was afraid she was overlooking something and wanted to talk to the screenwriter again. I knew if it was my wife, I'd be pretty concerned having her talking to people at night when a woman had died in the vicinity a few days earlier, and Sheriff, I'm sure you would have felt the same way.

"I asked Kelly if I could go with her, and she said yes. I told her I wanted to put Rusty in the house, but the truth is, I wanted to get the gun I keep in my nightstand and bring it with us. I had no idea what to expect. I've never had an occasion to use the gun, but I believe a man needs to be ready to defend his family and his property if it ever becomes necessary."

"Roger, wasn't your wife curious about what you were doing?" Kelly asked.

"No. When Chris gets involved in one of her television shows, I might as well not even be there. I don't like the kind of stuff she generally watches, so she wears earphones. I'll bet she didn't even hear the sirens. Anyway, I put the gun in my pocket, because, as I said, I wasn't sure what was going to happen. Fortunately, I didn't have to fire it. It's been a long time since I spent any time at a shooting range, and I have no idea how accurate my aim would have been."

"So, that's what I felt just before you yelled out to Teddy," Kelly said. "I felt a movement from you, but I didn't want to take my eyes away from what was going on to see what you were doing."

"Brandon, are you finished with their statements?" Mike asked.

"Yes, we have enough to arrest Teddy James for Jacquie Morton's murder. Sheriff, can you imagine the field day the media is going to have with this? Big time movie director murders big time movie star. Sounds almost like it ought to be a movie."

"I think Rebel and I better leave and try and get some sleep," Kelly said. "It's been so busy at the coffee shop all week, and now with this, there will probably be even more people coming to Cedar Bay. Even though tomorrow's Saturday and we're usually closed, I think I'll call the staff and open the coffe shop. I'd be willing to bet that we'll have plenty of customers."

She turned to Lisette and Mickey who were sitting on the couch. Mickey had his arm around her, and Lisette was quietly crying as she rested her head against his chest. "I don't know much about making movies, but it seems like The Triangle is one that was meant to be made. I wish you both good luck, and when it comes out, I'll be one of the first to buy a ticket." She smiled at them as she walked out the door, Mike by her side.

"Kelly, I need to go to the station. I'll be home late. Are you okay to drive?"

"I'm fine, Mike, and the good news is that since the mystery surrounding Jacquie's death has been solved, you're probably not going to have to work as a waiter at the coffee shop, because you're going to be re-elected." She grinned at him and turned to Roger.

"You'll never know how glad I am you happened to be standing outside when I walked by and you had the common sense to go inside your house and get your gun. You're a hero, and I thank you for keeping me safe, catching a murderer, and saving my husband's career. Next time you're in Cedar Bay, please stop by Kelly's Koffee Shop. Whatever you want is on the house. Rebel, come."

EPILOGUE

Lisette Andrews was nominated for an Academy Award as Best Actress for the film, The Triangle, and easily won it. Everyone said her performance was amazing. She's now one of the hottest stars in Hollywood. Teddy had been right about her becoming a star, and his prediction that she'd become a bigger star than Jacquie Morton might just come true, although it happened a little differently than he'd thought it would.

Mickey Sloan was nominated for an Academy Award as the screenwriter for the film, The Triangle, and won. He's very much in demand and can pick and choose which films he'll be involved in.

Lisette and Mickey recently got married in one of Tinseltown's largest weddings. Both were well-liked by the people in the film industry. When Teddy James found out that Lisette and Mickey were getting married, rumor has it that he had to be placed on suicide watch at the county jail where he's awaiting sentencing after being convicted for the murder of Jacquie Morton.

Kim and Jonah decided to get married with Guru Dev's blessing. She gave Guru Dev the majority of her inheritance, and the three of them are busy making plans to open more retreat centers in the Western United States.

Juan Hernandez received $100,000 as a gift from Kim. She and

Maizie talk often, and Maizie convinced her that while the money wouldn't make the tragedy the Hernandez family was facing go away, it would be a huge help to them in dealing with it.

Maizie Ortiz retired, bought a condominium in Portland, and lives a couple of blocks from her daughter and her family. She watches a lot of movies and tells people about all the celebrities she met when she was working for Jacquie Morton, the movie star who was murdered. She says she's never been happier.

Mike easily won re-election as the sheriff of Beaver County, Oregon. Not much has been heard from his opponent since the election.

Lem, Mike's campaign manager, breathed a big sigh of relief when Mike called him and told him Jacquie's murderer had been arrested. Lem doesn't think he'll get involved in any more campaigns. He wants to end his foray into politics on a high note with a win.

Kelly continues to run Kelly's Koffee Shop and enjoy her three four-legged furry children, not to be confused with her son, daughter, son-in-law, and granddaughters. It was pretty hectic in Cedar Bay for a long time, what with Jacquie Morton's murder and then the trial of Teddy, but things are finally back to normal.

Rebel's enjoying his time as the alpha dog in the Reynolds' household. He thinks Kelly still needs him, so every weekday when she goes to the door to leave for the coffee shop, he's waiting to go with her.

Skyy and Lady are only too happy to nap on either side of Rebel.

Roger Babowal is spending his days taking walks with Rusty and writing his life story for his children and grandchildren. He recently added a new chapter that deals with the part he played in capturing the murderer of the famous movie star, Jacquie Morton.

Life in Cedar Bay, the quiet little sleepy coastal town in Oregon, is back to normal.

RECIPES

MORNING MUFFINS

Muffin Ingredients:
1 ½ cups all-purpose flour
1 tsp. baking powder
1/8 tsp. baking soda
1 cup sugar
½ cup butter, unsalted and cut into pieces (Yes, you can use salted butter, but you have a lot more control of a recipe if you use unsalted butter)
2 eggs (I like to use jumbo size)
½ cup sour cream (I like to use regular, rather than lo-fat. Think it makes the muffins taste richer)
1 tsp. vanilla (Please don't use imitation. If you're going to spend the time making the recipe, buy authentic ingredients, not imitation – rant over!)

Streusel Topping Ingredients:
½ cup packed brown sugar
½ cup all-purpose flour
½ tsp. ground cinnamon
¼ cup cold, unsalted butter cut into pieces (You can read my

thoughts on unsalted butter above)

Muffin Directions:

Preheat oven to 400 degrees. Using a muffin tin containing 12 muffin cups, line the cups with paper muffin cups or spray with nonstick cooking spray. Combine flour, baking powder, baking soda and sugar in a food processor.

Pulse about three times. Sprinkle the butter over the dry ingredients and pulse until the mixture resembles small peas. Add eggs, sour cream and vanilla. Process for 30 seconds. Scrape the sides of the processor and resume processing until the mixture is blended. Put ¼ cup of the mixture in each muffin cup.

Streusel Topping Directions:

Put brown sugar, flour and cinnamon in a food processor and pulse to combine, then add the butter and pulse until the mixture resembles small peas. Top each muffin with 1 tbsp. of the mixture. Bake until golden, approximately 15 – 17 minutes. Enjoy!

NOTE: You can make the topping in advance and store it in the refrigerator.

MAKE-AHEAD FRENCH TOAST

Ingredients:

9 cups of bread with soft crusts (I prefer sourdough bread._
1 cup sugar
1 tsp. ground cinnamon
8 eggs (I like jumbo size)
2 cups heavy cream

Suggested Toppings (Choose Your Own):

Maple Syrup (Use real maple syrup. I know it costs more, but it's ever so much better than imitation syrup.)
Butter
Powdered sugar

Fresh fruit

Directions:

You can assemble this the day or the night before you plan to serve it. Tear the bread into 1" size pieces. Put the pieces in a large bowl. Mix the cinnamon and sugar in a small bowl. In a third bowl, whisk the eggs, cream, and ¼ cup of sugar-cinnamon mixture. Pour the mixture over the bread and stir until coated.

Preheat oven to 350 degrees. Spray a 9" x 13" glass baking dish with nonstick cooking spray. Spread the batter into the dish and top with the remaining sugar-cinnamon mixture. Bake until puffed and golden brown, about 45 minutes. Top with butter, powdered sugar and toppings. Enjoy!

NOTE: This really makes a lot. You may want to cut the recipe in half and adjust the baking time.

SAUSAGE & HASH BROWN CASSEROLE

Ingredients:

1 lb. bulk pork sausage
1 onion, chopped
8 eggs (I prefer the jumbo size), lightly beaten
½ cup flour
1 cup sour cream
6 scallions, chopped
1 tsp. dried sage
1 tsp. dried thyme
½ tsp. lemon pepper seasoning (I like Lawry's, but any brand will work)
½ cup milk
2 cups frozen shredded hash brown potatoes, defrosted (You can get these in the frozen food section of a supermarket)
1 ¼ cups shredded cheddar cheese

Directions:

Coat a 9" x 13" glass cooking dish or a muffin tin containing 12-muffin cups with nonstick cooking spray. In a large skillet, cook the sausage and onion. Break the meat apart into small bite-size pieces and cook until it's brown.

In a large bowl beat the eggs, flour, sour cream, scallions, sage, thyme, lemon pepper, and milk until blended. Fold in the cooked sausage and onion mixture, potatoes, and 1 cup of cheese. Pour in the prepared dish or muffin cups. Sprinkle the remaining cheese on top.

Preheat oven to 325 degrees. Bake until puffed and brown, about 25 – 35 minutes for the casserole, 15 – 20 minutes for the muffins. Let cool 5 minutes, serve, and enjoy!

NOTE: Can be made the day before and refrigerated. Bring to room temperature before baking.

CROCK POT CHILI WITH CILANTRO SOUR CREAM

Chili Ingredients:
2 lbs. lean ground beef
2 ¼ tsp. salt (I always prefer to use kosher salt when I'm making a savory dish)
Freshly ground black pepper to taste
1 tbsp. tomato paste
1 onion, chopped
1 cup red bell pepper, seeded and chopped
3 garlic cloves, minced
1 cup water
2 15 oz. cans beans (any combination of beans such as black, pinto, etc.)
1 10 oz. can diced tomatoes with green chilies
1 8 oz. can tomato sauce
2 tsp. ground cumin

1 to 3 tsp. chili powder (This totally depends on how hot you like your chili)
1 tsp. sweet paprika
½ tsp. garlic powder

Cilantro Sour Cream Ingredients:
½ cup sour cream
2 tbsp. chopped fresh cilantro
¼ tsp. ground cumin
1 tsp. freshly squeezed lime juice
Optional Topping Ingredients:
½ cup grated cheddar cheese
1/3 cup chopped red onion

Chili Directions:
In a large deep skillet over medium high heat, cook ground beef, salt, and pepper to taste until no trace of pink remains. (I like to use a wooden spoon to break up the beef into bite-size pieces.)

Add the remaining ingredients to the cooked meat, combine, and then transfer the mixture to a slow cooker or crock pot. Cover and cook on high for 5 hours or on low for 7 – 9 hours.

Cilantro Sour Cream Directions:
Combine sour cream, cilantro, cumin, and lime juice. Cover and refrigerate until ready to serve.

Ladle chili into bowls and let each person top with the cilantro sour cream and/or other toppings. Enjoy!

FUDGY BROWNIES

Ingredients:
5 tbsp. unsalted butter (Use the unsalted rather than the salted), cut into 5 pieces
4 oz. semisweet chocolate, chopped
2 oz. unsweetened chocolate, chopped

¾ cup sugar
¼ tsp. salt
2 eggs (I prefer jumbo size)
½ cup all-purpose flour
 12 oz. chocolate chips
1 cup walnut pieces (optional – my grandchildren don't like nuts, so I don't put them in, if you have people who like nuts, go ahead!)
Tin foil
2 tbsp. softened butter

Directions:
Preheat oven to 325 degrees. Place a metal bowl over a pan of water which has been brought to a simmer. Put the butter in the bowl and top with the chocolate. Heat until melted. Remove from heat and stir in sugar and salt.

Whisk in the eggs, one at a time until the mixture is smooth. Add the flour. Gently stir in the chocolate chips and walnuts, if desired. Pour the mixture into an 8" x 8" glass baking dish and bake for 40 - 45 minutes. Remove from oven and place the dish on a wire cooling rack. When the brownies are cool, cut into pieces. Enjoy!

NOTE: My husband says he's had millions of brownies (which I believe is a slight exaggeration, and these are the best he's ever had.) That's a pretty good testimonial.

Paperbacks & Ebooks for FREE

Go to www.dianneharman.com/freepaperback.html and get your FREE copies of Dianne's books and favorite recipes immediately by signing up for her newsletter.

Once you've signed up for her newsletter you're eligible to win three paperbacks. One lucky winner is picked every week. Hurry before the offer ends!

ABOUT THE AUTHOR

Dianne lives in Huntington Beach, California, with her husband, Tom, a former California State Senator, and her boxer dog, Kelly. Her passions are cooking, reading, and dogs, so whenever she has a little free time, you can either find her in the kitchen, playing with Kelly in the back yard, or curled up with the latest book she's reading.

Her award winning books include:

Cedar Bay Cozy Mystery Series
Kelly's Koffee Shop, Murder at Jade Cove, White Cloud Retreat, Marriage and Murder, Murder in the Pearl District, Murder in Calico Gold, Murder at the Cooking School, Murder in Cuba, Trouble at the Kennel, Murder on the East Coast, Trouble at the Animal Shelter, Murder & The Movie Star

Liz Lucas Cozy Mystery Series
Murder in Cottage #6, Murder & Brandy Boy, The Death Card, Murder at The Bed & Breakfast, The Blue Butterfly, Murder at the Big T Lodge, Murder in Calistoga

High Desert Cozy Mystery Series
Murder & The Monkey Band, Murder & The Secret Cave, Murdered by Country Music, Murder at the Polo Club

Midwest Cozy Mystery Series
Murdered by Words, Murder at the Clinic

Jack Trout Cozy Mystery Series
Murdered in Argentina

Northwest Cozy Mystery Series
Murder on Bainbridge Island

Coyote Series
Blue Coyote Motel, Coyote in Provence, Cornered Coyote

Midlife Journey Series
Alexis

Website: www.dianneharman.com, **Blog:** www.dianneharman.com/blog
Email: dianne@dianneharman.com

Newsletter

If you would like to be notified of her latest releases please go to www.dianneharman.com and sign up for her newsletter.

Made in United States
Orlando, FL
28 November 2022

25158797R00081